THE

TEMPLE SHAKESPEARE

By the kind permission of Messrs Macmillan & Co.
and W. Aldis Wright, Esq., the text here
used is that of the "Cambridge" Edition.

First Edition of this issue of "Much Ado about Nothing" printed June 1894.
Second Edition, August 1894. Third Edition, January 1895. Fourth Edition,
November 1896. Fifth Edition, February 1898. Sixth Edition, February
1899. Seventh Edition, April 1900. Eighth Edition, December 1900. Ninth
Edition, March 1902. Tenth Edition, March 1903. Eleventh Edition,
October 1904. Twelfth Edition, January 1906.

Holy Trinity Church
Stratford on Avon

Now STRATFORD-UPON-AVON, we would choose
Thy gentle and ingenuous SHAKESPEARE Muse
     *   *   *   *   *
Our WARWICKSHIRE the heart of England is,
As you must evidently have prov'd by this:
Having it with more spirit dignifi'd,
Than all our English Counties are beside.

   SIR ASTON COKAIN, 1658 (to William Dugdale's
       WARWICKSHIRE ILLUSTRATED.)

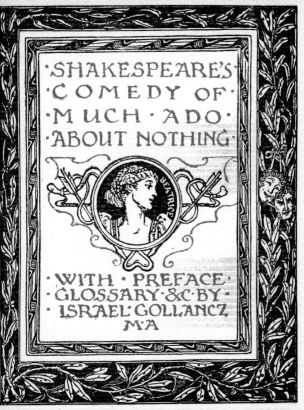

SHAKESPEARE'S
COMEDY OF
MUCH ADO
ABOUT NOTHING

BEATRICE

WITH PREFACE
GLOSSARY &C BY
ISRAEL GOLLANCZ
M A

LONDON: PUBLISHED BY J M DENT
AND CO: ALDINE HOUSE W C: MCMVI

"THE interest in the plot is always on account of the characters, not *vice versa*, as in almost all other writers; the plot is a mere canvas and no more. Hence arises the true justification of the same stratagem being used in regard to Benedick and Beatrice,—the vanity in each being alike. Take away from the 'Much Ado About Nothing' all that which is not indispensable to the plot, either as having little to do with it, or, at best, like Dogberry and his comrades, forced into the service, when any other less ingeniously absurd watchmen and night-constables would have answered the mere necessities of the action;—take away Benedick, Beatrice, Dogberry, and the reaction of the former on the character of Hero,—and what will remain? In other writers the main agent of the plot is always the prominent character; in Shakspere it is so, or is not so, as the character is in itself calculated, or not calculated, to form the plot. Don John is the mainspring of the plot of this play; but he is merely shown and then withdrawn."

COLERIDGE.

Preface.

The Editions. A quarto edition of *Much Ado About Nothing* was published in 1600 with the following title-page:—' *Much Adoe About Nothing as it hath been sundrie times publikely acted by the right honourable the Lord Chamberlain his servants Written by William Shakespeare.* London.' (It had previously been entered on the Stationers' Register, August 23, 1600.) No other edition is known to have been published previous to the publication of the First Folio, 1623; the play was evidently printed from a copy of a Quarto in the possession of the Theatre, or of the original MS., corrected for the purposes of the Stage. (*Cp. Facsimile Quarto Edition*, ed. by Mr Daniel.) There are many minor variations between the Quarto and the First Folio, but most of them seem due to the printer's carelessness.

Date of Composition. As the play is not mentioned by Meres, in 1598, and was printed in 1600, it may be safely assigned to the year 1599, in support of which date the following points are noteworthy:—(1) Probable allusion in the opening scene to a circumstance attending the campaign of the Earl of Essex in Ireland, during the summer of 1599; (2) the character of "Amorphus, or the one Deformed," in *Cynthia's Revels*, 1600, may be compared with "the one Deformed, a vile thief this seven year" (*cp.* III. iii. 133-5, 182, 185); (3) the instructions which Dogberry and Verges give to the night-watch may possibly be intended as

v

a burlesque on *The Statutes of the Streets*, imprinted by Wolfe, in 1595.

Source of Plot. The incident of the interrupted marriage is identical with the story of Ariodante and Ginevra in Ariosto's *Orlando Furioso*, canto v.; this had been translated into English by Beverly in 1565, and by Harrington in 1591. The story was dramatised before 1582, and was rendered into English verse by George Turbervile. Later on it found a place in Spenser's *Fairy Queen*, Book ii. Canto iv. Shakespeare may, however, have derived his story from Belleforest's translation in his *Histoires Tragiques* of Bandello's 22nd Novella. It is noteworthy that about the same time the German Dramatist, Jacob Ayrer, founded his play *Beautiful Phænicia* upon the same tale, and the English and German plays have certain points of resemblance. Possibly they were both indebted to a lost original (*cp.* Cohn's *Shakespeare in Germany*). Dr Ward sums up the evidence as follows:—" As the date of Ayrer's piece is not known—it may have been written before or after 1600—and as that of Shakspere's is similarly uncertain, it is impossible to decide as to their relative priority. That, however, Ayrer did not copy from Shakspere seems, as Simrock points out, clear from the names of the characters in his play, which follow Bandello, while Shakspere has changed all the names except those of Don Pedro and old Leonato."

General Characteristics. The mixture of tragedy and comedy in this play is so perfectly blended that it may well be regarded as the culminating point of Shakespeare's second period of activity, the period to which belongs *Twelfth Night*, *As You Like It*, and *The Merry Wives*; the metrical tests actually place it last in this group. Beatrice and Benedick should be compared with their prototypes Rosaline and Biron, and Dogberry and his comrades should be contrasted with the earlier clowns, in order to understand the advance which this play marks in Shakespeare's career. "Perhaps," says Hazlitt, "the middle point of comedy was never more nicely hit, in which the ludicrous blends with the tender, and our follies, turning round against themselves, in support of our affections, retain nothing but their humanity."

Later Versions of the Play. Two plays were founded upon *Much Ado About Nothing*—(1) Davenant's *Law against Lovers*, which Pepys saw on Feb. 18th, 1661, and (2) *The Universal Passion*, by Rev. James Miller, 1737.

Duration of Action. For a detailed study of the "time" of the play the reader is referred to Mr Daniel's "Time-Analysis," *Trans. of New Shaks. Soc.* 1877-79, p. 144. He believes that just as the Prince forgets his determination to stay "at least a month" at Messina, so the "just seven-night" to the wedding was also either forgotten or intentionally set aside, and that only four *consecutive* days are actually included in the action of the drama—

1. Act I., and Act II. i. and ii.
2. Act II. iii., and Act III. i.-iii.
3. Act III. iv. and v.; Act IV.; Act V. i. ii., and part of iii.
4. Act V., part of iii., and iv.

DRAMATIS PERSONÆ.

DON PEDRO, *prince of Arragon.*
DON JOHN, *his bastard brother.*
CLAUDIO, *a young lord of Florence.*
BENEDICK, *a young lord of Padua.*
LEONATO, *governor of Messina.*
ANTONIO, *his brother.*
BALTHASAR, *attendant on Don Pedro.*
CONRADE, }
BORACHIO, } *followers of Don John.*
FRIAR FRANCIS.
DOGBERRY, *a constable.*
VERGES, *a headborough*
A SEXTON.
A BOY.

HERO, *daughter to Leonato.*
BEATRICE, *niece to Leonato.*
MARGARET, }
URSULA, } *gentlewomen attending on Hero.*

Messengers, Watch, Attendants, &c.

SCENE, *Messina.*

Much Ado about Nothing.

Act First.

Scene I.

Before Leonato's house.

Enter Leonato, Hero, and Beatrice, with a Messenger.

Leon. I learn in this letter that Don Pedro of Arragon comes this night to Messina.

Mess. He is very near by this: he was not three leagues off when I left him.

Leon. How many gentlemen have you lost in this action?

Mess. But few of any sort, and none of name.

Leon. A victory is twice itself when the achiever brings home full numbers. I find here that Don Pedro hath bestowed much honour on 10 a young Florentine called Claudio.

Mess. Much deserved on his part, and equally remembered by Don Pedro: he hath borne him-

1

self beyond the promise of his age; doing, in
the figure of a lamb, the feats of a lion: he hath
indeed better bettered expectation than you
must expect of me to tell you how.

Leon. He hath an uncle here in Messina will be
very much glad of it.

Mess. I have already delivered him letters, and   20
there appears much joy in him; even so much,
that joy could not show itself modest enough
without a badge of bitterness.

Leon. Did he break out into tears?

Mess. In great measure.

Leon. A kind overflow of kindness: there are no
faces truer than those that are so washed. How
much better is it to weep at joy than to joy at
weeping!

Beat. I pray you, is Signior Mountanto returned   30
from the wars or no?

Mess. I know none of that name, lady: there was
none such in the army of any sort.

Leon. What is he that you ask for, niece?

Hero. My cousin means Signior Benedick of
Padua.

Mess. O, he's returned; and as pleasant as ever
he was.

2

Beat. He set up his bills here in Messina and
    challenged Cupid at the flight; and my uncle's   40
    fool, reading the challenge, subscribed for Cupid,
    and challenged him at the bird-bolt. I pray
    you, how many hath he killed and eaten in these
    wars? But how many hath he killed? for, in-
    deed, I promised to eat all of his killing.

Leon. Faith, niece, you tax Signior Benedick too
    much; but he'll be meet with you, I doubt it not.

Mess. He hath done good service, lady, in these
    wars.

Beat. You had musty victual, and he hath holp to   50
    eat it: he is a very valiant trencher-man; he
    hath an excellent stomach.

Mess. And a good soldier too, lady.

Beat. And a good soldier to a lady; but what is he
    to a lord?

Mess. A lord to a lord, a man to a man; stuffed
    with all honourable virtues.

Beat. It is so, indeed; he is no less than a stuffed
    man: but for the stuffing,—well, we are all
    mortal.   60

Leon. You must not, sir, mistake my niece. There
    is a kind of merry war betwixt Signior Benedick

and her : they never meet but there's a skirmish
of wit between them.

Beat. Alas! he gets nothing by that. In our last
conflict four of his five wits went halting off, and
now is the whole man governed with one : so
that if he have wit enough to keep himself warm,
let him bear it for a difference between himself
and his horse ; for it is all the wealth that he 70
hath left, to be known a reasonable creature.
Who is his companion now ? He hath every
month a new sworn brother.

Mess. Is't possible ?

Beat. Very easily possible : he wears his faith but as
the fashion of his hat ; it ever changes with the
next block.

Mess. I see, lady, the gentleman is not in your
books.

Beat. No ; an he were, I would burn my study. 80
But, I pray you, who is his companion ? Is
there no young squarer now that will make a
voyage with him to the devil ?

Mess. He is most in the company of the right noble
Claudio.

Beat. O Lord, he will hang upon him like a disease :
he is sooner caught than the pestilence, and the

    taker runs presently mad.   God help the noble
    Claudio ! if he have caught the Benedick, it will
    cost him a thousand pound ere a' be cured.   90

Mess. I will hold friends with you, lady.

Beat. Do, good friend.

Leon. You will never run mad, niece.

Beat. No, not till a hot January.

Mess. Don Pedro is approached.

> *Enter Don Pedro, Don John, Claudio, Benedick,*
>   *and Balthasar.*

D. Pedro. Good Signior Leonata, you are come to
    meet your trouble : the fashion of the world is
    to avoid cost, and you encounter it.

Leon. Never came trouble to my house in the like-
    ness of your Grace : for trouble being gone,   100
    comfort should remain ; but when you depart from
    me, sorrow abides, and happiness takes his leave.

D. Pedro. You embrace your charge too willingly.
    I think this is your daughter.

Leon. Her mother hath many times told me so.

Bene. Were you in doubt, sir, that you asked
    her ?

Leon. Signior Benedick, no ; for then were you a
    child.

D. Pedro. You have it full, Benedick: we may 110
guess by this what you are, being a man. Truly,
the lady fathers herself. Be happy, lady; for
you are like an honourable father.

Bene. If Signior Leonato be her father, she would
not have his head on her shoulders for all
Messina, as like him as she is.

Beat. I wonder that you will still be talking, Signior
Benedick: nobody marks you.

Bene. What, my dear Lady Disdain! are you yet
living? 120

Beat. Is it possible disdain should die while she hath
such meet food to feed it, as Signior Benedick?
Courtesy itself must convert to disdain, if you
come in her presence

Bene. Then is courtesy a turncoat. But it is certain
I am loved of all ladies, only you excepted: and
I would I could find in my heart that I had not
a hard heart; for, truly, I love none.

Beat. A dear happiness to women: they would else
have been troubled with a pernicious suitor. I 130
thank God and my cold blood, I am of your
humour for that: I had rather hear my dog bark
at a crow than a man swear he loves me.

Bene. God keep your ladyship still in that mind! so

some gentleman or other shall 'scape a pre-
destinate scratched face.

Beat. Scratching could not make it worse, an 'twere
such a face as yours were.

Bene. Well, you are a rare parrot-teacher.

Beat. A bird of my tongue is better than a beast of 140
yours.

Bene. I would my horse had the speed of your
tongue, and so good a continuer. But keep
your way, i' God's name; I have done.

Beat. You always end with a jade's trick: I know
you of old.

D. Pedro. That is the sum of all, Leonato. Signior
Claudio and Signior Benedick, my dear friend
Leonata hath invited you all. I tell him we
shall stay here at the least a month; and he 150
heartily prays some occasion may detain us
longer. I dare swear he is no hypocrite, but
prays from his heart.

Leon. If you swear, my lord, you shall not be for-
sworn. [*To Don John*] Let me bid you
welcome, my lord: being reconciled to the
prince your brother, I owe you all duty.

D. John. I thank you: I am not of many words,
but I thank you.

7

Leon. Please it your Grace lead on? 160

D. Pedro. Your hand, Leonato; we will go together.   [*Exeunt all except Benedick and Claudio.*

Claud. Benedick, didst thou note the daughter of Signior Leonato?

Bene. I noted her not; but I looked on her.

Claud. Is she not a modest young lady?

Bene. Do you question me, as an honest man should do, for my simple true judgement? or would you have me speak after my custom, as being a professed tyrant to their sex? 170

Claud. No; I pray thee speak in sober judgement.

Bene. Why, i' faith, methinks she's too low for a high praise, too brown for a fair praise, and too little for a great praise: only this commendation I can afford her, that were she other than she is, she were unhandsome; and being no other but as she is, I do not like her.

Claud. Thou thinkest I am in sport: I pray thee tell me truly how thou likest her. 180

Bene. Would you buy her, that you inquire after her?

Claud. Can the world buy such a jewel?

Bene. Yea, and a case to put it into. But speak

you this with a sad brow? or do you play the
flouting Jack, to tell us Cupid is a good hare-
finder, and Vulcan a rare carpenter? Come, in
what key shall a man take you, to go in the song?

Claud. In mine eye she is the sweetest lady that
ever I looked on.   190

Bene. I can see yet without spectacles, and I see no
such matter: there's her cousin, an she were
not possessed with a fury, exceeds her as much
in beauty as the first of May doth the last of
December. But I hope you have no intent
to turn husband, have you?

Claud. I would scarce trust myself, though I had
sworn the contrary, if Hero would be my wife.

Bene. Is't come to this? In faith, hath not the
world one man but he will wear his cap with 200
suspicion? Shall I never see a bachelor of
threescore again? Go to, i' faith; an thou wilt
needs thrust thy neck into a yoke, wear the
print of it, and sigh away Sundays. Look;
Don Pedro is returned to seek you.

Re-enter Don Pedro.

D. Pedro. What secret hath held you here, that you
followed not to Leonato's?

Bene. I would your Grace would constrain me to
　　tell.

D. Pedro. I charge thee on thy allegiance.　　　　210

Bene. You hear, Count Claudio : I can be secret as
　　a dumb man ; I would have you think so ; but,
　　on my allegiance, mark you this, on my allegi-
　　ance.　He is in love.　With who ? now that
　　is your Grace's part.　Mark how short his an-
　　swer is ;—With Hero, Leonato's short daughter.

Claud. If this were so, so were it uttered.

Bene. Like the old tale, my lord : ' it is not so, nor
　　'twas not so, but, indeed, God forbid it should
　　be so.'　　　　　　　　　　　　　　　　220

Claud. If my passion change not shortly, God forbid
　　it should be otherwise.

D. Pedro. Amen, if you love her ; for the lady is
　　very well worthy.

Claud. You speak this to fetch me in, my lord.

D. Pedro. By my troth, I speak my thought.

Claud. And, in faith, my lord, I spoke mine.

Bene. And, by my two faiths and troths, my lord,
　　I spoke mine.

Claud. That I love her, I feel.　　　　　　　230

D. Pedro. That she is worthy, I know.

Bene. That I neither feel how she should be loved,

nor know how she should be worthy, is the opinion that fire cannot melt out of me : I will die in it at the stake.

D. Pedro. Thou wast ever an obstinate heretic in the despite of beauty.

Claud. And never could maintain his part but in the force of his will.

Bene. That a woman conceived me, I thank her ; 240 that she brought me up, I likewise give her most humble thanks : but that I will have a recheat winded in my forehead, or hang my bugle in an invisible baldrick, all women shall pardon me. Because I will not do them the wrong to mistrust any, I will do myself the right to trust none ; and the fine is, for the which I may go the finer, I will live a bachelor.

D. Pedro. I shall see thee, ere I die, look pale with love. 250

Bene. With anger, with sickness, or with hunger, my lord ; not with love : prove that ever I lose more blood with love than I will get again with drinking, pick out mine eyes with a ballad-maker's pen, and hang me up at the door of a brothel-house for the sign of blind Cupid.

D. Pedro. Well, if ever thou dost fall from this
faith, thou wilt prove a notable argument.

Bene. If I do, hang me in a bottle like a cat, and
shoot at me ; and he that hits me, let him be 260
clapped on the shoulder and called Adam.

D. Pedro. Well, as time shall try :
' In time the savage bull doth bear the yoke.'

Bene. The savage bull may ; but if ever the sensible
Benedick bear it, pluck off the bull's horns,
and set them in my forehead : and let me be
vilely painted ; and in such great letters as they
write ' Here is good horse to hire,' let them
signify under my sign ' Here you may see Benedick the married man.'   270

Claud. If this should ever happen, thou wouldst be
horn-mad.

D. Pedro. Nay, if Cupid have not spent all his quiver
in Venice, thou wilt quake for this shortly.

Bene. I look for an earthquake too, then.

D. Pedro. Well, you will temporize with the hours.
In the meantime, good Signior Benedick, repair
to Leonato's : commend me to him, and tell
him I will not fail him at supper ; for indeed he
hath made great preparation.   280

Bene. I have almost matter enough in me for such
     an embassage ; and so I commit you—

Claud. To the tuition of God : From my house,
     if I had it,—

D. Pedro. The sixth of July : Your loving friend,
     Benedick.

Bene. Nay, mock not, mock not. The body of your
     discourse is sometime guarded with fragments,
     and the guards are but slightly basted on neither:
     ere you flout old ends any further, examine your 290
     conscience : and so I leave you.   [*Exit.*

Claud. My liege, your highness now may do me good.

D. Pedro. My love is thine to teach : teach it but how,
     And thou shalt see how apt it is to learn
     Any hard lesson that may do thee good.

Claud. Hath Leonato any son, my lord ?

D. Pedro. No child but Hero ; she 's his only heir.
     Dost thou affect her, Claudio ?

Claud.   O, my lord,
     When you went onward on this ended action,
     I look'd upon her with a soldier's eye,   300
     That liked, but had a rougher task in hand
     Than to drive liking to the name of love :
     But now I am return'd and that war-thoughts
     Have left their places vacant, in their rooms

Come thronging soft and delicate desires,
All prompting me how fair young Hero is,
Saying, I liked her ere I went to wars.

D. Pedro. Thou wilt be like a lover presently,
And tire the hearer with a book of words.
If thou dost love fair Hero, cherish it;   310
And I will break with her and with her father,
And thou shalt have her. Was 't not to this end
That thou began'st to twist so fine a story?

Claud. How sweetly you do minister to love,
That know love's grief by his complexion!
But lest my liking might too sudden seem,
I would have salved it with a longer treatise.

D. Pedro. What need the bridge much broader than the
    flood?
The fairest grant is the necessity.
Look, what will serve is fit: 'tis once, thou lovest,
And I will fit thee with the remedy.   321
I know we shall have revelling to-night:
I will assume thy part in some disguise,
And tell fair Hero I am Claudio;
And in her bosom I 'll unclasp my heart,
And take her hearing prisoner with the force
And strong encounter of my amorous tale:
Then after to her father will I break;

And the conclusion is, she shall be thine.
In practice let us put it presently.   [*Exeunt.* 330

Scene II.

A room in Leonato's house
Enter Leonato and Antonio, meeting.

Leon. How now, brother! Where is my cousin,
     your son? hath he provided this music?

Ant. He is very busy about it. But, brother, I can
     tell you strange news, that you yet dreamt not
     of.

Leon. Are they good?

Ant. As the event stamps them: but they have a
     good cover; they show well outward. The
     prince and Count Claudio, walking in a thick-
     pleached alley in mine orchard, were thus much   10
     overheard by a man of mine: the prince dis-
     covered to Claudio that he loved my niece your
     daughter, and meant to acknowledge it this
     night in a dance; and if he found her accordant,
     he meant to take the present time by the top,
     and instantly break with you of it.

Leon. Hath the fellow any wit that told you
     this?

Ant. A good sharp fellow: I will send for him;
　and question him yourself.　　　　　　　　20
Leon. No, no; we will hold it as a dream till it
　appear itself: but I will acquaint my daughter
　withal, that she may be the better prepared for
　an answer, if peradventure this be true.　Go you
　and tell her of it.　[*Enter attendants.*]　Cou-
　sins, you know what you have to do.　O, I
　cry you mercy, friend; go you with me, and I
　will use your skill.　Good cousin, have a care
　this busy time.　　　　　　　　　　[*Exeunt.*

Scene III.

The same.

Enter Don John and Conrade.

Con. What the good-year, my lord! why are you
　thus out of measure sad?
D. John. There is no measure in the occasion that
　breeds; therefore the sadness is without
　limit.
Con. You should hear reason.
D. John. And when I have heard it, what blessing
　brings it?

Con. If not a present remedy, at least a patient
    sufferance.   10

D. John. I wonder that thou, being (as thou sayest
    thou art) born under Saturn, goest about to apply
    a moral medicine to a mortifying mischief. I
    cannot hide what I am: I must be sad when I
    have cause, and smile at no man's jests; eat
    when I have stomach, and wait for no man's
    leisure; sleep when I am drowsy, and tend on
    no man's business; laugh when I am merry,
    and claw no man in his humour.

Con. Yea, but you must not make the full show of   20
    this till you may do it without controlment. You
    have of late stood out against your brother, and
    he hath ta'en you newly into his grace; where
    it is impossible you should take true root but by
    the fair weather that you make yourself: it is
    needful that you frame the season for your own
    harvest.

D. John. I had rather be a canker in a hedge than a
    rose in his grace; and it better fits my blood to
    be disdained of all than to fashion a carriage to   30
    rob love from any: in this, though I cannot be
    said to be a flattering honest man, it must not be
    denied but I am a plain-dealing villain. I am

> trusted with a muzzle, and enfranchised with a
> clog; therefore I have decreed not to sing in
> my cage. If I had my mouth, I would bite;
> if I had my liberty, I would do my liking: in
> the meantime let me be that I am, and seek not
> to alter me.

Con. Can you make no use of your discontent?   40

D. John. I make all use of it, for I use it only.
     Who comes here?

Enter Borachio.

What news, Borachio?

Bora. I came yonder from a great supper: the prince
     your brother is royally entertained by Leonato;
     and I can give you intelligence of an intended
     marriage.

D. John. Will it serve for any model to build mis-
     chief on? What is he for a fool that betroths
     himself to unquietness?   50

Bora. Marry, it is your brother's right hand.

D. John. Who? the most exquisite Claudio?

Bora. Even he.

D. John. A proper squire! And who, and who?
     which way looks he?

Bora. Marry, on Hero, the daughter and heir of
    Leonato.

D. John. A very forward March-chick! How
    came you to this?

Bora. Being entertained for a perfumer, as I was   60
    smoking a musty room, comes me the prince
    and Claudio, hand in hand, in sad conference:
    I whipt me behind the arras; and there heard
    it agreed upon, that the prince should woo Hero
    for himself, and having obtained her, give her
    to Count Claudio.

D John. Come, come, let us thither: this may prove
    food to my displeasure. That young start-up
    hath all the glory of my overthrow: if I can
    cross him any way, I bless myself every way.   70
    You are both sure, and will assist me?

Con. To the death, my lord.

D. John. Let us to the great supper: their cheer
    is the greater that I am subdued. Would the
    cook were of my mind! Shall we go prove
    what's to be done?

Bora. We'll wait upon your lordship.   [*Exeunt.*

Act Second.

Scene I.

A hall in Leonato's house.

Enter Leonato, Antonio, Hero, Beatrice, and others.

Leon. Was not Count John here at supper?

Ant. I saw him not.

Beat. How tartly that gentleman looks! I never can see him but I am heart-burned an hour after.

Hero. He is of a very melancholy disposition.

Beat. He were an excellent man that were made just in the midway between him and Benedick: the one is too like an image and says nothing, and the other too like my lady's eldest son, evermore tattling. 　10

Leon. Then half Signior Benedick's tongue in Count John's mouth, and half Count John's melancholy in Signior Benedick's face,—

Beat. With a good leg and a good foot, uncle, and money enough in his purse, such a man would win any woman in the world, if a' could get her good-will.

Leon. By my troth, niece, thou wilt never get
thee a husband, if thou be so shrewd of thy 20
tongue.

Ant. In faith, she's too curst.

Beat. Too curst is more than curst: I shall lessen
God's sending that way; for it is said, 'God
sends a curst cow short horns;' but to a cow
too curst he sends none.

Leon. So, by being too curst, God will send you no
horns.

Beat. Just, if he send me no husband; for the which
blessing I am at him upon my knees every 30
morning and evening. Lord, I could not endure a husband with a beard on his face: I had
rather lie in the woollen.

Leon. You may light on a husband that hath no
beard.

Beat. What should I do with him? dress him in my
apparel, and make him my waiting-gentlewoman?
He that hath a beard is more than a youth; and
he that hath no beard is less than a man: and
he that is more than a youth is not for me; and 40
he that is less than a man, I am not for him:
therefore I will even take sixpence in earnest of
the bear-ward, and lead his apes into hell.

Leon. Well, then, go you into hell?

Beat. No, but to the gate; and there will the devil
meet me, like an old cuckold, with horns on his
head, and say 'Get you to heaven, Beatrice,
get you to heaven; here's no place for you
maids:' so deliver I up my apes, and away to
Saint Peter for the heavens; he shows me   50
where the bachelors sit, and there live we as
merry as the day is long.

Ant. [*To Hero*] Well, niece, I trust you will be
ruled by your father.

Beat. Yes, faith; it is my cousin's duty to make
courtesy, and say, 'Father, as it please you.'
But yet for all that, cousin, let him be a handsome fellow, or else make another courtesy, and
say, 'Father, as it please me.'

Leon. Well, niece, I hope to see you one day fitted   60
with a husband.

Beat. Not till God make men of some other metal
than earth. Would it not grieve a woman to
be overmastered with a piece of valiant dust?
to make an account of her life to a clod of way-
ward marl? No, uncle, I'll none: Adam's
sons are my brethren; and, truly, I hold it a
sin to match in my kindred.

Leon. Daughter, remember what I told you: if the prince do solicit you in that kind, you know 70 your answer.

Beat. The fault will be in the music, cousin, if you be not wooed in good time: if the prince be too important, tell him there is measure in every thing, and so dance out the answer. For, hear me, Hero: wooing, wedding, and repenting, is as a Scotch jig, a measure, and a cinque pace: the first suit is hot and hasty, like a Scotch jig, and full as fantastical; the wedding, mannerly-modest, as a measure, full of state and ancientry; 80 and then comes repentance, and, with his bad legs, falls into the cinque pace faster and faster, till he sink into his grave.

Leon. Cousin, you apprehend passing shrewdly.

Beat. I have a good eye, uncle; I can see a church by daylight.

Leon. The revellers are entering, brother: make good room.   [*All put on their masks.*

Enter Don Pedro, Claudio, Benedick, Balthasar, Don John, Borachio, Margaret, Ursula, and others, masked.

D. Pedro. Lady, will you walk about with your friend? 90

Hero. So you walk softly, and look sweetly, and
    say nothing, I am yours for the walk; and
    especially when I walk away.

D. Pedro. With me in your company?

Hero. I may say so, when I please.

D. Pedro. And when please you to say so?

Hero. When I like your favour; for God defend
    the lute should be like the case!

D. Pedro. My visor is Philemon's roof; within the
    house is Jove.   100

Hero. Why, then, your visor should be
    thatched.

D. Pedro. Speak low, if you speak love.

                [Drawing her aside.

Balth. Well, I would you did like me.

Marg. So would not I, for your own sake; for I
    have many ill qualities.

Balth. Which is one?

Marg. I say my prayers aloud.

Balth. I love you the better: the hearers may cry,
    Amen.   110

Marg. God match me with a good dancer!

Balth. Amen.

Marg. And God keep him out of my sight when
    the dance is done! Answer, clerk.

Balth. No more words: the clerk is answered.

Urs. I know you well enough; you are Signior
  Antonio.

Ant. At a word, I am not.

Urs. I know you by the waggling of your
  head.   120

Ant. To tell you true, I counterfeit him.

Urs. You could never do him so ill-well, unless you
  were the very man. Here's his dry hand up
  and down: you are he, you are he.

Ant. At a word, I am not.

Urs. Come, come, do you think I do not know you
  by your excellent wit? can virtue hide itself?
  Go to, mum, you are he: graces will appear,
  and there's an end.

Beat. Will you not tell me who told you so?   130

Bene. No, you shall pardon me.

Beat. Nor will you not tell me who you are?

Bene. Not now.

Beat. That I was disdainful, and that I had my
  good wit out of the 'Hundred Merry Tales':
  —well, this was Signior Benedick that said so.

Bene. What's he?

Beat. I am sure you know him well enough.

Bene. Not I, believe me.

Beat. Did he never make you laugh?　　　　　140
Bene. I pray you, what is he?
Beat. Why, he is the prince's jester: a very dull
　　fool; only his gift is in devising impossible
　　slanders: none but libertines delight in him;
　　and the commendation is not in his wit, but in
　　his villany; for he both pleases men and angers
　　them, and then they laugh at him and beat him.
　　I am sure he is in the fleet: I would he had
　　boarded me.
Bene. When I know the gentleman, I 'll tell him　150
　　what you say.
Beat. Do, do: he 'll but break a comparison or two
　　on me; which, peradventure not marked or not
　　laughed at, strikes him into melancholy; and
　　then there 's a partridge wing saved, for the fool
　　will eat no supper that night. [*Music.*] We
　　must follow the leaders.
Bene. In every good thing.
Beat. Nay, if they lead to any ill, I will leave them
　　at the next turning.　　　　　160

　　　　　　[*Dance. Then exeunt all except Don John,
　　　　　　　　Borachio, and Claudio.*

D. John. Sure my brother is amorous on Hero, and
　　hath withdrawn her father to break with him

about it. The ladies follow her, and but one
visor remains.

Bora. And that is Claudio: I know him by his
bearing.

D. John. Are not you Signior Benedick?

Claud. You know me well; I am he.

D. John. Signior, you are very near my brother in
his love; he is enamoured on Hero; I pray 170
you, dissuade him from her: she is no equal
for his birth: you may do the part of an honest
man in it.

Claud. How know you he loves her?

D. John. I heard him swear his affection.

Bora. So did I too; and he swore he would marry
her to-night.

D. John. Come, let us to the banquet.

                     [*Exeunt Don John and Borachio.*

Claud. Thus answer I in name of Benedick,
But hear these ill news with the ears of Claudio. 180
'Tis certain so; the prince wooes for himself.
Friendship is constant in all other things
Save in the office and affairs of love:
Therefore all hearts in love use their own tongues;
Let every eye negotiate for itself,
And trust no agent; for beauty is a witch,

Against whose charms faith melteth into blood.
This is an accident of hourly proof,
Which I mistrusted not. Farewell, therefore, Hero!

Re-enter Benedick.

Bene. Count Claudio?   190
Claud. Yea, the same.
Bene. Come, will you go with me?
Claud. Whither?
Bene. Even to the next willow, about your own busi-
ness, county. What fashion will you wear the
garland of? about your neck, like an usurer's
chain? or under your arm, like a lieutenant's
scarf? You must wear it one way, for the prince
hath got your Hero.
Claud. I wish him joy of her.   200
Bene. Why, that's spoken like an honest drovier; so
they sell bullocks. But did you think the
prince would have served you thus?
Claud. I pray you, leave me.
Bene. Ho! now you strike like the blind man;
'twas the boy that stole your meat, and you'll
beat the post.
Claud. If it will not be, I'll leave you.   [*Exit.*
Bene. Alas, poor hurt fowl! now will he creep into

28

sedges. But, that my lady Beatrice should 210
know me, and not know me! The prince's fool!
Ha? It may be I go under that title because I
am merry. Yea, but so I am apt to do myself
wrong; I am not so reputed: it is the base,
though bitter, disposition of Beatrice that puts
the world into her person, and so gives me out.
Well, I'll be revenged as I may.

Re-enter Don Pedro.

D. Pedro. Now, signior, where's the count? did
you see him?

Bene. Troth, my lord, I have played the part of Lady 220
Fame. I found him here as melancholy as a
lodge in a warren: I told him, and I think I
told him true, that your grace had got the good
will of this young lady; and I offered him my
company to a willow-tree, either to make him a
garland, as being forsaken, or to bind him up a
rod, as being worthy to be whipped.

D. Pedro. To be whipped! What's his fault?

Bene. The flat transgression of a school-boy, who,
being overjoyed with finding a birds' nest, shows 230
it his companion, and he steals it,

D. Pedro. Wilt thou make a trust a transgression ?
The transgression is in the stealer.

Bene. Yet it had not been amiss the rod had been
made, and the garland too ; for the garland he
might have worn himself, and the rod he might
have bestowed on you, who, as I take it, have
stolen his birds' nest.

D. Pedro. I will but teach them to sing, and restore
them to the owner.   240

Bene. If their singing answer your saying, by my
faith, you say honestly.

D. Pedro. The Lady Beatrice hath a quarrel to you:
the gentleman that danced with her told her she
is much wronged by you.

Bene. O, she misused me past the endurance of a
block ! an oak but with one green leaf on it
would have answered her ; my very visor began
to assume life and scold with her. She told me,
not thinking I had been myself, that I was the   250
prince's jester, that I was duller than a great
thaw ; huddling jest upon jest, with such impossible conveyance, upon me, that I stood like a
man at a mark, with a whole army shooting at
me. She speaks poniards, and every word stabs:
if her breath were as terrible as her terminations,

there were no living near her ; she would infect
to the north star. I would not marry her,
though she were endowed with all that Adam
had left him before he transgressed : she would 260
have made Hercules have turned spit, yea, and
have cleft his club to make the fire too. Come,
talk not of her: you shall find her the infernal Ate
in good apparel. I would to God some scholar
would conjure her; for certainly, while she is here,
a man may live as quiet in hell as in a sanctuary ;
and people sin upon purpose, because they would
go thither ; so, indeed, all disquiet, horror, and
perturbation follows her.

D. Pedro. Look, here she comes.   270

Re-enter Claudio, Beatrice, Hero, and Leonato.

Bene. Will your grace command me any service to
the world's end ? I will go on the slightest
errand now to the Antipodes that you can devise to send me on ; I will fetch you a tooth-
picker now from the furthest inch of Asia; bring
you the length of Prester John's foot ; fetch you
a hair off the great Cham's beard ; do you any
embassage to the Pigmies; rather than hold three

words' conference with this harpy. You have
no employment for me? 280

D. Pedro. None, but to desire your good company.

Bene. O God, sir, here's a dish I love not: I cannot endure my Lady Tongue. [*Exit.*

D. Pedro. Come, lady, come; you have lost the
heart of Signior Benedick.

Beat. Indeed, my lord, he lent it me awhile; and
I gave him use for it, a double heart for his
single one: marry, once before he won it of me
with false dice, therefore your Grace may well 290
say I have lost it.

D. Pedro. You have put him down, lady, you have
put him down.

Beat. So I would not he should do me, my lord,
lest I should prove the mother of fools. I
have brought Count Claudio, whom you sent
me to seek.

D. Pedro. Why, how now, count! wherefore are
you sad?

Claud. Not sad, my lord. 300

D. Pedro. How then? sick?

Claud. Neither, my lord.

Beat. The count is neither sad, nor sick, nor
merry, nor well; but civil count, civil as an

orange, and something of that jealous complexion.

D. Pedro. I' faith, lady, I think your blazon to be
true ; though, I 'll be sworn, if he be so, his
conceit is false. Here, Claudio, I have wooed in
thy name, and fair Hero is won : I have broke 310
with her father, and his good will obtained :
name the day of marriage, and God give thee joy!

Leon. Count, take of me my daughter, and with her
my fortunes : his Grace hath made the match,
and all grace say Amen to it.

Beat. Speak, count, 'tis your cue.

Claud. Silence is the perfectest herald of joy : I
were but little happy, if I could say how much.
Lady, as you are mine, I am yours : I give away
myself for you, and dote upon the exchange. 320

Beat. Speak, cousin ; or, if you cannot, stop his
mouth with a kiss, and let not him speak
neither.

D. Pedro. In faith, lady, you have a merry
heart.

Beat. Yea, my lord ; I thank it, poor fool, it keeps
on the windy side of care. My cousin tells
him in his ear that he is in her heart.

Claud. And so she doth, cousin.

Beat. **Good** Lord, for alliance! Thus goes every 330
one to the world but I, and I am sun-burnt;
I may sit in a corner, and cry heigh-ho for a
husband!

D. Pedro. Lady Beatrice, I will get you one.

Beat. I would rather have one of your father's
getting. Hath your Grace ne'er a brother like
you? Your father got excellent husbands, if a
maid could come by them.

D. Pedro. Will you have me, lady?

Beat. No, my lord, unless I might have another for 340
working-days: your Grace is too costly to
wear every day. But, I beseech your Grace,
pardon me: I was born to speak all mirth and
no matter.

D. Pedro. Your silence most offends me, and to be
merry best becomes you; for, out of question,
you were born in a merry hour.

Beat. No, sure, my lord, my mother cried; but then
there was a star danced, and under that was I
born. Cousins, God give you joy! 350

Leon. Niece, will you look to those things I told
you of?

Beat. I cry you mercy, uncle. By your Grace's
pardon, [*Exit.*

D. Pedro. By my troth, a pleasant - spirited
     lady.

Leon. There's little of the melancholy element in
     her, my lord: she is never sad but when she
     sleeps; and not ever sad then; for I have
     heard my daughter say, she hath often dreamed 360
     of unhappiness, and waked herself with laughing.

D. Pedro. She cannot endure to hear tell of a
     husband.

Leon. O, by no means: she mocks all her wooers
     out of suit.

D. Pedro. She were an excellent wife for
     Benedick.

Leon. O Lord, my lord, if they were but a week
     married, they would talk themselves mad.

D. Pedro. County Claudio, when mean you to go 370
     to church?

Claud. To-morrow, my lord: time goes on crutches
     till love have all his rites.

Leon. Not till Monday, my dear son, which is hence
     a just seven-night; and a time too brief, too,
     to have all things answer my mind.

D. Pedro. Come, you shake the head at so long a
     breathing: but, I warrant thee, Claudio, the
     time shall not go dully by us. I will, in the

interim, undertake one of Hercules' labours ; 380
which is, to bring Signior Benedick and the
Lady Beatrice into a mountain of affection the
one with the other. I would fain have it a
match ; and I doubt not but to fashion it, if you
three will but minister such assistance as I shall
give you direction.

Leon. My lord, I am for you, though it cost me ten
nights' watchings.

Claud. And I, my lord.

D. Pedro. And you too, gentle Hero ?

Hero. I will do any modest office, my lord, to help 390
my cousin to a good husband.

D. Pedro. And Benedick is not the unhopefullest
husband that I know. Thus far can I praise
him ; he is of a noble strain, of approved valour,
and confirmed honesty. I will teach you how
to humour your cousin, that she shall fall in love
with Benedick ; and I, with your two helps,
will so practise on Benedick, that, in despite of
his quick wit and his queasy stomach, he shall
fall in love with Beatrice. If we can do this, 400
Cupid is no longer an archer : his glory shall
be ours, for we are the only love-gods. Go in
with me, and I will tell you my drift. [*Exeunt.*

Scene II.

The same.

Enter Don John and Borachio.

D. John. It is so ; the Count Claudio shall marry
    the daughter of Leonato.

Bora. Yea, my lord ; but I can cross it.

D. John. Any bar, any cross, any impediment will be
    medicinable to me : I am sick in displeasure to
    him ; and whatsoever comes athwart his affec-
    tion ranges evenly with mine.   How canst thou
    cross this marriage ?

Bora. Not honestly, my lord ; but so covertly that
    no dishonesty shall appear in me.   10

D. John. Show me briefly how.

Bora. I think I told your lordship, a year since, how
    much I am in the favour of Margaret, the
    waiting gentlewoman to Hero.

D. John. I remember.

Bora. I can, at any unseasonable instant of the night,
    appoint her to look out at her lady's chamber
    window.

D. John. What life is in that, to be the death of this
    marriage ?   20

Bora. The poison of that lies in you to temper. Go
  you to the prince your brother ; spare not to tell
  him that he hath wronged his honour in marry-
  ing the renowned Claudio—whose estimation do
  you mightily hold up—to a contaminated stale,
  such a one as Hero.

D. John. What proof shall I make of that ?

Bora. Proof enough to misuse the prince, to vex
  Claudio, to undo Hero, and kill Leonato.
  Look you for any other issue ?   30

D. John. Only to despite them I will endeavour any
  thing.

Bora. Go, then ; find me a meet hour to draw Don
  Pedro and the Count Claudio alone : tell them
  that you know that Hero loves me ; intend a
  kind of zeal both to the prince and Claudio, as,
  —in love of your brother's honour, who hath
  made this match, and his friend's reputation, who
  is thus like to be cozened with the semblance of
  a maid,—that you have discovered thus. They   40
  will scarcely believe this without trial: offer them
  instances ; which shall bear no less likelihood
  than to see me at her chamber-window ; hear
  me call Margaret, Hero ; hear Margaret term
  me Claudio ; and bring them to see this the

very night before the intended wedding,—for in the meantime I will so fashion the matter that Hero shall be absent,—and there shall appear such seeming truth of Hero's disloyalty, that jealousy shall be called assurance and all the   50 preparation overthrown.

D. John. Grow this to what adverse issue it can, I will put it in practice. Be cunning in the working this, and thy fee is a thousand ducats.

Bora. Be you constant in the accusation, and my cunning shall not shame me.

D. John. I will presently go learn their day of marriage.   [*Exeunt.*

Scene III.

Leonato's orchard.

Enter Benedick.

Bene. Boy!

Enter Boy.

Boy. Signior?

Bene. In my chamber-window lies a book: bring it hither to me in the orchard.

Boy. I am here already, sir.

Bene. I know that; but I would have thee hence,
and here again. [*Exit Boy.*] I do much
wonder that one man, seeing how much another
man is a fool when he dedicates his behaviours to
love, will, after he hath laughed at such shallow   10
follies in others, become the argument of his
own scorn by falling in love: and such a man is
Claudio. I have known when there was no
music with him but the drum and the fife; and
now had he rather hear the tabor and the pipe:
I have known when he would have walked ten
mile a-foot to see a good armour; and now will
he lie ten nights awake, carving the fashion of a
new doublet. He was wont to speak plain and
to the purpose, like an honest man and a soldier;   20
and now is he turned orthography; his words are
a very fantastical banquet,—just so many strange
dishes. May I be so converted, and see with
these eyes? I cannot tell; I think not: I will not
be sworn but love may transform me to an oyster;
but I'll take my oath on it, till he have made
an oyster of me, he shall never make me such
a fool. One woman is fair, yet I am well;
another is wise, yet I am well; another virtuous,
yet I am well: but till all graces be in one woman,   30

40

one woman shall not come in my grace. Rich
she shall be, that's certain; wise, or I'll none;
virtuous, or I'll never cheapen her; fair, or
I'll never look on her; mild, or come not near
me; noble, or not I for an angel; of good discourse, an excellent musician, and her hair shall
be of what colour it please God. Ha! the prince
and Monsieur Love! I will hide me in the arbour.

                           [Withdraws.

Enter Don Pedro, Claudio, and Leonato.

D. Pedro. Come, shall we hear this music?
Claud. Yea, my good lord. How still the evening is, 40
    As hush'd on purpose to grace harmony!
D. Pedro. See you where Benedick hath hid himself?
Claud. O, very well, my lord: the music ended,
    We'll fit the kid-fox with a pennyworth.

Enter Balthasar with Music.

D. Pedro. Come, Balthasar, we'll hear that song again.
Balth. O, good my lord, tax not so bad a voice
    To slander music any more than once.
D. Pedro. It is the witness still of excellency
    To put a strange face on his own perfection.
    I pray thee, sing, and let me woo no more.   50

Balth. Because you talk of wooing, I will sing;
Since many a wooer doth commence his suit
To her he thinks not worthy, yet he wooes,
Yet will he swear he loves.

D. Pedro.　　　　　　　Nay, pray thee, come;
Or, if thou wilt hold longer argument,
Do it in notes.

Balth.　　　　　Note this before my notes;
There's not a note of mine that's worth the noting.

D. Pedro. Why, these are very crotchets that he speaks;
Note, notes, forsooth, and nothing.　　　　*[Air.*

Bene. Now, divine air! now is his soul ravished! Is 60
it not strange that sheeps' guts should hale souls
out of men's bodies? Well, a horn for my
money, when all's done.

The Song.

Balth.　　Sigh no more, ladies, sigh no more,
　　　　Men were deceivers ever,
　　One foot in sea and one on shore,
　　　　To one thing constant never:
　　Then sigh not so, but let them go,
　　　　And be you blithe and bonny,
　　Converting all your sounds of woe　　　70
　　　　Into Hey nonny, nonny.

42

> Sing no more ditties, sing no moe,
>   Of dumps so dull and heavy ;
> The fraud of men was ever so,
>   Since summer first was leavy :
>   Then sigh not so, &c.

D. Pedro. By my troth, a good song.

Balth. And an ill singer, my lord.

D. Pedro. Ha, no, no, faith ; thou singest well enough for a shift.   80

Bene. An he had been a dog that should have howled thus, they would have hanged him : and I pray God his bad voice bode no mischief. I had as lief have heard the night-raven, come what plague could have come after it.

D. Pedro. Yea, marry, dost thou hear, Balthasar ? I pray thee, get us some excellent music ; for to-morrow night we would have it at the Lady Hero's chamber-window.

Balth. The best I can, my lord.   90

D. Pedro. Do so : farewell. [*Exit Balthasar.*] Come hither, Leonato. What was it you told me of to-day, that your niece Beatrice was in love with Signior Benedick ?

Claud. O, ay : stalk on, stalk on ; the fowl sits. I

did never think that lady would have loved any man.

Leon. No, nor I neither; but most wonderful that she should so dote on Signior Benedick, whom she hath in all outward behaviours seemed ever 100 to abhor.

Bene. Is 't possible? Sits the wind in that corner?

Leon. By my troth, my lord, I cannot tell what to think of it, but that she loves him with an enraged affection; it is past the infinite of thought.

D. Pedro. May be she doth but counterfeit.

Claud. Faith, like enough.

Leon. O God, counterfeit! There was never counterfeit of passion came so near the life of 110 passion as she discovers it.

D. Pedro. Why, what effects of passion shows she?

Claud. Bait the hook well; this fish will bite.

Leon. What effects, my lord? She will sit you, you heard my daughter tell you how.

Claud. She did, indeed.

D. Pedro. How, how, I pray you? You amaze me: I would have thought her spirit had been invincible against all assaults of affection. 120

44

Leon. I would have sworn it had, my lord; especially
    against Benedick.

Bene. I should think this a gull, but that the white-
    bearded fellow speaks it : knavery cannot, sure,
    hide himself in such reverence.

Claud. He hath ta'en the infection : hold it up.

D. Pedro. Hath she made her affection known to
    Benedick ?

Leon. No ; and swears she never will : that's her
    torment.   130

Claud. 'Tis true, indeed; so your daughter says :
    ' Shall I,' says she, ' that have so oft encountered
    him with scorn, write to him that I love
    him ? '

Leon. This says she now when she is beginning to
    write to him; for she 'll be up twenty times a
    night; and there will she sit in her smock till
    she have writ a sheet of paper : my daughter
    tells us all.

Claud. Now you talk of a sheet of paper, I remember   140
    a pretty jest your daughter told us of.

Leon. O, when she had writ it, and was reading it
    over, she found Benedick and Beatrice between
    the sheet ?

Claud. That.

Leon. O, she tore the letter into a thousand half-
pence; railed at herself, that she should be so
immodest to write to one that she knew would
flout her; 'I measure him,' says she, 'by my
own spirit; for I should flout him, if he writ 150
to me; yea, though I love him, I should.'

Claud. Then down upon her knees she falls, weeps,
sobs, beats her heart, tears her hair, prays,
curses; 'O sweet Benedick! God give me
patience!'

Leon. She doth indeed; my daughter says so: and
the ecstasy hath so much overborne her, that
my daughter is sometime afeard she will do a
desperate outrage to herself: it is very true.

D. Pedro. It were good that Benedick knew of it by 160
some other, if she will not discover it.

Claud. To what end? He would make but a sport
of it, and torment the poor lady worse.

D. Pedro. An he should, it were an alms to hang
him. She 's an excellent sweet lady; and, out
of all suspicion, she is virtuous.

Claud. And she is exceeding wise.

D. Pedro. In every thing but in loving Benedick.

Leon. O, my lord, wisdom and blood combating in so 170

46

tender a body, we have ten proofs to one that
blood hath the victory. I am sorry for her,
as I have just cause, being her uncle and her
guardian.

D. Pedro. I would she had bestowed this dotage on
me : I would have daffed all other respects, and
made her half myself. I pray you, tell Benedick of it, and hear what a' will say.

Leon. Were it good, think you ?

Claud. Hero thinks surely she will die ; for she says 180
she will die, if he love her not ; and she will
die, ere she make her love known ; and she will
die, if he woo her, rather than she will bate one
breath of her accustomed crossness.

D. Pedro. She doth well : if she should make
tender of her love, 'tis very possible he 'll scorn
it ; for the man, as you know all, hath a contemptible spirit.

Claud. He is a very proper man.

D. Pedro. He hath indeed a good outward happi- 190
ness.

Claud. Before God ! and in my mind, very wise.

D. Pedro. He doth indeed show some sparks that
are like wit.

Claud. And I take him to be valiant.

D. Pedro. As Hector, I assure you: and in the
    managing of quarrels you may say he is wise;
    for either he avoids them with great discretion,
    or undertakes them with a most Christian-like
    fear.   200

Leon. If he do fear God, a' must necessarily keep
    peace: if he break the peace, he ought to enter
    into a quarrel with fear and trembling.

D. Pedro. And so will he do; for the man doth
    fear God, howsoever it seems not in him by
    some large jests he will make. Well, I am
    sorry for your niece. Shall we go seek Bene-
    dick, and tell him of her love?

Claud. Never tell him, my lord: let her wear it out
    with good counsel.

Leon. Nay, that's impossible: she may wear her
    heart out first.   210

D. Pedro. Well, we will hear further of it by your
    daughter: let it cool the while. I love Bene-
    dick well; and I could wish he would modestly
    examine himself, to see how much he is unworthy
    so good a lady.

Leon. My lord, will you walk? dinner is ready.

Claud. If he do not dote on her upon this, I will
    never trust my expectation.   220

D. Pedro. Let there be the same net spread for
her; and that must your daughter and her
gentlewomen carry. The sport will be, when
they hold one an opinion of another's dotage,
and no such matter: that's the scene that I
would see, which will be merely a dumb-show.
Let us send her to call him in to dinner.

[*Exeunt Don Pedro, Claudio, and Leonato.*

Bene. [*Coming forward*] This can be no trick:
the conference was sadly borne. They have
the truth of this from Hero. They seem to 230
pity the lady: it seems her affections have their
full bent. Love me! why, it must be requited.
I hear how I am censured: they say I will bear
myself proudly, if I perceive the love come from
her; they say too that she will rather die than
give any sign of affection. I did never think to
marry: I must not seem proud: happy are they
that hear their detractions, and can put them to
mending. They say the lady is fair,—'tis a
truth, I can bear them witness; and virtuous,— 240
'tis so, I cannot reprove it; and wise, but for
loving me,—by my troth, it is no addition to her
wit, nor no great argument of her folly, for I
will be horribly in love with her. I may chance

have some odd quirks and remnants of wit broken
on me, because I have railed so long against marriage : but doth not the appetite alter ? a man
loves the meat in his youth that he cannot endure
in his age.　Shall quips and sentences and these
paper bullets of the brain awe a man from the 250
career of his humour ?　No, the world must be
peopled.　When I said I would die a bachelor,
I did not think I should live till I were married.
Here comes Beatrice.　By this day ! she's a
fair lady : I do spy some marks of love in her.

Enter Beatrice.

Beat. Against my will I am sent to bid you come in
　　to dinner.

Bene. Fair Beatrice, I thank you for your pains.

Beat. I took no more pains for those thanks than
　　you take pains to thank me : if it had been 260
　　painful, I would not have come.

Bene. You take pleasure, then, in the message ?

Beat. Yea, just so much as you may take upon a
　　knife's point, and choke a daw withal.　You
　　have no stomach, signior : fare you well.　　[*Exit.*

Bene. Ha ! 'Against my will I am sent to bid you
　　come in to dinner ;' there's a double meaning

in that. ‘ I took no more pains for those thanks
than you took pains to thank me ; ’ that ’s as
much as to say, Any pains that I take for you 270
is as easy as thanks.   If I do not take pity of
her, I am a villain ; if I do not love her, I am
a Jew.   I will go get her picture.   [*Exit.*

Act Third.

Scene I.

Leonato’s orchard.

Enter Hero, Margaret, and Ursula

Hero. Good Margaret, run thee to the parlour
There shalt thou find my cousin Beatrice
Proposing with the prince and Claudio :
Whisper her ear, and tell her, I and Ursula
Walk in the orchard, and our whole discourse
Is all of her ; say that thou overheard’st us ;
And bid her steal into the pleached bower,
Where honeysuckles, ripen’d by the sun,
Forbid the sun to enter ; like favourites,
Made proud by princes, that advance their pride 10

Against that power that bred it : there will she hide
      her,
To listen our propose.   This is thy office ;
Bear thee well in it, and leave us alone.
Marg. I'll make her come, I warrant you, presently. [*Exit.*
Hero. Now, Ursula, when Beatrice doth come,
      As we do trace this alley up and down,
      Our talk must only be of Benedick.
      When I do name him, let it be thy part
      To praise him more than ever man did merit :
      My talk to thee must be, how Benedick   20
      Is sick in love with Beatrice.   Of this matter
      Is little Cupid's crafty arrow made,
      That only wounds by hearsay.

              Enter Beatrice, behind.

                            Now begin ;
      For look where Beatrice, like a lapwing, runs
      Close by the ground, to hear our conference.
Urs. The pleasant'st angling is to see the fish
      Cut with her golden oars the silver stream,
      And greedily devour the treacherous bait :
      So angle we for Beatrice ; who even now
      Is couched in the woodbine coverture.   30
      Fear you not my part of the dialogue.

Hero. Then go we near her, that her ear lose nothing
    Of the false sweet bait that we lay for it.
                             [Approaching the bower.
    No, truly, Ursula, she is too disdainful;
    I know her spirits are as coy and wild
    As haggerds of the rock.

Urs.   But are you sure
    That Benedick loves Beatrice so entirely?

Hero. So says the prince and my new-trothed lord.

Urs. And did they bid you tell her of it, madam?

Hero. They did entreat me to acquaint her of it;   40
    But I persuaded them, if they loved Benedick,
    To wish him wrestle with affection,
    And never to let Beatrice know of it.

Urs. Why did you so? Doth not the gentleman
    Deserve as full as fortunate a bed
    As ever Beatrice shall couch upon?

Hero. O god of love! I know he doth deserve
    As much as may be yielded to a man:
    But Nature never framed a woman's heart
    Of prouder stuff than that of Beatrice;   50
    Disdain and scorn ride sparkling in her eyes,
    Misprising what they look on; and her wit
    Values itself so highly, that to her
    All matter else seems weak: she cannot love,

Nor take no shape nor project of affection,
She is so self-endeared.

Urs.   Sure, I think so ;
And therefore certainly it were not good
She knew his love, lest she make sport at it.

Hero. Why, you speak truth. I never yet saw man,
How wise, how noble, young, how rarely featured, 60
But she would spell him backward : if fair-faced,
She would swear the gentleman should be her sister ;
If black, why, Nature, drawing of an antique,
Made a foul blot ; if tall, a lance ill-headed ;
If low, an agate very vilely cut ;
If speaking, why, a vane blown with all winds ;
If silent, why, a block moved with none.
So turns she every man the wrong side out ;
And never gives to truth and virtue that
Which simpleness and merit purchaseth.   70

Urs. Sure, sure, such carping is not commendable.

Hero. No, not to be so odd, and from all fashions,
As Beatrice is, cannot be commendable :
But who dare tell her so ? If I should speak,
She would mock me into air; O, she would laugh me
Out of myself, press me to death with wit !
Therefore let Benedick, like cover'd fire,
Consume away in sighs, waste inwardly :

It were a better death than die with mocks,
Which is as bad as die with tickling.   80

Urs. Yet tell her of it: hear what she will say.

Hero. No; rather I will go to Benedick,
And counsel him to fight against his passion.
And, truly, I'll devise some honest slanders
To stain my cousin with: one doth not know
How much an ill word may empoison liking.

Urs. O, do not do your cousin such a wrong!
She cannot be so much without true judgement,—
Having so swift and excellent a wit
As she is prized to have,—as to refuse   90
So rare a gentleman as Signior Benedick.

Hero. He is the only man of Italy,
Always excepted my dear Claudio.

Urs. I pray you, be not angry with me, madam,
Speaking my fancy: Signior Benedick,
For shape, for bearing, argument and valour,
Goes foremost in report through Italy.

Hero. Indeed, he hath an excellent good name.

Urs. His excellence did earn it, ere he had it.
When are you married, madam?   100

Hero. Why, every day, to-morrow. Come, go in:
I'll show thee some attires; and have thy counsel
Which is the best to furnish me to-morrow.

Urs. She's limed, I warrant you: we have caught her,
    madam.

Hero. If it prove so, then loving goes by haps:
    Some Cupid kills with arrows, some with traps.

                       [*Exeunt Hero and Ursula.*

Beat. [*Coming forward*] What fire is in mine ears?
    Can this be true?

    Stand I condemn'd for pride and scorn so much?
  Contempt, farewell! and maiden pride, adieu!
    No glory lives behind the back of such.   110
  And, Benedick, love on; I will requite thee,
    Taming my wild heart to thy loving hand:
  If thou dost love, my kindness shall incite thee
    To bind our loves up in a holy band;
  For others say thou dost deserve, and I
  Believe it better than reportingly.   [*Exit.*

Scene II.

A room in Leonato's house.

Enter Don Pedro, Claudio, Benedick, and Leonato.

D. Pedro. I do but stay till your marriage be con-
    summate, and then go I toward Arragon.

Claud. I 'll bring you thither, my lord, if you 'll
    vouchsafe me.

D. Pedro. Nay, that would be as great a soil in the
new gloss of your marriage, as to show a child
his new coat and forbid him to wear it.   I will
only be bold with Benedick for his company ;
for, from the crown of his head to the sole of
his foot, he is all mirth : he hath twice or thrice   10
cut Cupid's bow-string, and the little hangman
dare not shoot at him ; he hath a heart as sound
as a bell, and his tongue is the clapper, for what
his heart thinks his tongue speaks.

Bene. Gallants, I am not as I have been.

Leon. So say I : methinks you are sadder.

Claud. I hope he be in love.

D. Pedro. Hang him, truant ! there 's no true drop
of blood in him, to be truly touched with love ;
if he be sad, he wants money.   20

Bene. I have the toothache.

D. Pedro. Draw it.

Bene. Hang it !

Claud. You must hang it first, and draw it afterwards.

D. Pedro. What ! sigh for the toothache ?

Leon. Where is but a humour or a worm.

Bene. Well, every one can master a grief but he that
has it.

Claud. Yet say I, he is in love.　　　30

D. Pedro. There is no appearance of fancy in him, unless it be a fancy that he hath to strange disguises ; as, to be a Dutchman to-day, a Frenchman to-morrow ; or in the shape of two countries at once, as, a German from the waist downward, all slops, and a Spaniard from the hip upward, no doublet. Unless he have a fancy to this foolery, as it appears he hath, he is no fool for fancy, as you would have it appear he is.

Claud. If he be not in love with some woman, there　40 is no believing old signs : a' brushes his hat o' mornings ; what should that bode ?

D. Pedro. Hath any man seen him at the barber's ?

Claud. No, but the barber's man hath been seen with him ; and the old ornament of his cheek hath already stuffed tennis-balls.

Leon. Indeed, he looks younger than he did, by the loss of a beard.

D. Pedro. Nay, a' rubs himself with civet : can you　50 smell him out by that ?

Claud. That 's as much as to say, the sweet youth's in love.

D. Pedro. The greatest note of it is his melancholy.　58

Claud. And when was he wont to wash his
    face ?

D. Pedro. Yea, or to paint himself ? for the which,
    I hear what they say of him.

Claud. Nay, but his jesting spirit ; which is now   60
    crept into a lute-string, and now governed by
    stops.

D. Pedro. Indeed, that tells a heavy tale for him :
    conclude, conclude he is in love.

Claud. Nay, but I know who loves him.

D. Pedro. That would I know too : I warrant, one
    that knows him not.

Claud. Yes, and his ill conditions ; and, in despite
    of all, dies for him.

D. Pedro. She shall be buried with her face up-   70
    wards.

Bene. Yet is this no charm for the toothache. Old
    signior, walk aside with me : I have studied
    eight or nine wise words to speak to you, which
    these hobby-horses must not hear.

                         [Exeunt Benedick and Leonato.

D. Pedro. For my life, to break with him about
    Beatrice.

Claud. 'Tis even so. Hero and Margaret have by
    this played their parts with Beatrice ; and then

the two bears will not bite one another when 80
they meet.

Enter Don John.

D. John. My lord and brother, God save you!

D. Pedro. Good den, brother.

D. John. If your leisure served, I would speak with you.

D. Pedro. In private

D. John. If it please you: yet Count Claudio may hear; for what I would speak of concerns him.

D. Pedro. What's the matter? 90

D. John. [*To Claudio*] Means your lordship to be married to-morrow?

D. Pedro. You know he does.

D. John. I know not that, when he knows what I know.

Claud. If there be any impediment, I pray you discover it.

D. John. You may think I love you not: let that appear hereafter, and aim better at me by that I now will manifest. For my brother, I think he 100 holds you well, and in dearness of heart hath holp to effect your ensuing marriage,—surely suit ill spent and labour ill bestowed.

D. Pedro. Why, what's the matter?

D. John. I came hither to tell you; and, circumstances shortened, for she has been too long a
talking of, the lady is disloyal.

Claud. Who, Hero?

D. John. Even she; Leonato's Hero, your Hero,
every man's Hero.   110

Claud. Disloyal?

D. John. The word is too good to paint out her
wickedness; I could say she were worse. think
you of a worse title, and I will fit her to it.
Wonder not till further warrant: go but with me
to-night, you shall see her chamber-window entered,
even the night before her wedding-day: if you
love her then, to-morrow wed her; but it would
better fit your honour to change your mind.

Claud. May this be so?   120

D. Pedro. I will not think it.

D. John. If you dare not trust that you see, confess
not that you know: if you will follow me, I
will show you enough; and when you have
seen more, and heard more, proceed accordingly.

Claud. If I see any thing to-night why I should not
marry her to-morrow, in the congregation,
where I should wed, there will I shame her.

D. Pedro. And, as I wooed for thee to obtain her,
    I will join with thee to disgrace her.   130

D. John. I will disparage her no farther till you are
    my witnesses : bear it coldly but till midnight,
    and let the issue show itself.

D. Pedro. O day untowardly turned !

Claud. O mischief strangely thwarting !

D. John. O plague right well prevented ! so will
    you say when you have seen the sequel.   [*Exeunt.*

Scene III,

A street.

Enter Dogberry and Verges with the Watch.

Dog. Are you good men and true ?

Verg. Yea, or else it were pity but they should suffer
    salvation, body and soul.

Dog. Nay, that were a punishment too good for
    them, if they should have any allegiance in
    them, being chosen for the prince's watch.

Verg. Well, give them their charge, neighbour
    Dogberry.

Dog. First, who think you the most desartless man
    to be constable ?   10

First Watch. Hugh Otecake, sir, or George Seacole;
    for they can write and read.

Dog. Come hither, neighbour Seacole. God hath
    blessed you with a good name: to be a well-
    favoured man is the gift of fortune; but to
    write and read comes by nature.

Sec. Watch. Both which, master constable,—

Dog. You have: I knew it would be your answer.
    Well, for your favour, sir, why, give God
    thanks, and make no boast of it; and for your   20
    writing and reading, let that appear when there
    is no need of such vanity. You are thought
    here to be the most senseless and fit man for the
    constable of the watch; therefore bear you the
    lantern. This is your charge: you shall com-
    prehend all vagrom men; you are to bid any
    man stand, in the prince's name.

Sec. Watch. How if a' will not stand?

Dog. Why, then, take no note of him, but let him
    go; and presently call the rest of the watch   30
    together, and thank God you are rid of a knave.

Verg. If he will not stand when he is bidden, he is
    none of the prince's subjects.

Dog. True, and they are to meddle with none but
    the prince's subjects. You shall also make no

noise in the streets; for for the watch to babble
and to talk is most tolerable and not to be en-
dured.

Watch. We will rather sleep than talk: we know
what belongs to a watch.   40

Dog. Why, you speak like an ancient and most
quiet watchman; for I cannot see how sleeping
should offend: only, have a care that your bills
be not stolen. Well, you are to call at all
the ale-houses, and bid those that are drunk
get them to bed.

Watch. How if they will not?

Dog. Why, then, let them alone till they are
sober: if they make you not then the better
answer, you may say they are not the men you   50
took them for.

Watch. Well, sir.

Dog. If you meet a thief, you may suspect him,
by virtue of your office, to be no true man; and,
for such kind of men, the less you meddle or
make with them, why, the more is for your honesty.

Watch. If we know him to be a thief, shall we not
lay hands on him?

Dog. Truly, by your office, you may; but I think
they that touch pitch will be defiled: the most   60

peaceable way for you, if you do take a thief,
is to let him show himself what he is, and
steal out of your company.

Verg. You have been always called a merciful man,
partner.

Dog. Truly, I would not hang a dog by my will,
much more a man who hath any honesty in
him.

Verg. If you hear a child crying in the night, you
must call to the nurse and bid her still it.   70

Watch. How if the nurse be asleep and will not
hear us ?

Dog. Why, then, depart in peace, and let the child
wake her with crying; for the ewe that will
not hear her lamb when it baes will never
answer a calf when he bleats.

Verg. 'Tis very true.

Dog. This is the end of the charge:—you, constable, are to present the prince's own person;
if you meet the prince in the night, you may   80
stay him.

Verg. Nay, by'r lady, that I think a'
cannot.

Dog. Five shillings to one on't, with any man
that knows the statues, he may stay him:

marry, not without the prince be willing; for, indeed, the watch ought to offend no man; and it is an offence to stay a man against his will.

Verg. By 'r lady, I think it be so.

Dog. Ha, ah, ha! Well, masters, good night: an 90 there be any matter of weight chances, call up me: keep your fellows' counsels and your own; and good night. Come, neighbour.

Watch. Well, masters, we hear our charge: let us go sit here upon the church-bench till two, and then all to bed.

Dog. One word more, honest neighbours. I pray you, watch about Signior Leonato's door; for the wedding being there to-morrow, there is a great coil to-night. Adieu: be vigitant, I 100 beseech you.   [*Exeunt Dogberry and Verges.*

Enter Borachio and Conrade.

Bora. What, Conrade!

Watch. [*Aside*] Peace! stir not.

Bora. Conrade, I say!

Con. Here, man; I am at thy elbow.

Bora. Mass, and my elbow itched; I thought there would a scab follow.

Con. I will owe thee an answer for that: and now forward with thy tale.

Bora. Stand thee close, then, under this pent-house, 110
for it drizzles rain; and I will, like a true
drunkard, utter all to thee.

Watch. [*Aside*] Some treason, masters: yet stand
close.

Bora. Therefore know I have earned of Don John
a thousand ducats.

Con. Is it possible that any villany should be so
dear?

Bora. Thou shouldst rather ask, if it were possible
any villany should be so rich; for when rich 120
villains have need of poor ones, poor ones may
make what price they will.

Con. I wonder at it.

Bora. That shows thou art unconfirmed. Thou
knowest that the fashion of a doublet, or a hat,
or a cloak, is nothing to a man.

Con. Yes, it is apparel.

Bora. I mean, the fashion.

Con. Yes, the fashion is the fashion.

Bora. Tush! I may as well say the fool's the fool. 130
But seest thou not what a deformed thief this
fashion is?

Watch. [*Aside*] I know that Deformed; a' has
been a vile thief this seven year; a' goes up

and down like a gentleman: I remember his
name.

Bora. Didst thou not hear somebody?

Con. No; 'twas the vane on the house

Bora. Seest thou not, I say, what a deformed thief
this fashion is? how giddily a' turns about all 140
the hot bloods between fourteen and five-and-
thirty? sometimes fashioning them like Pharaoh's
soldiers in the reechy painting, sometime like god
Bel's priests in the old church-window, sometime like the shaven Hercules in the smirched
worm-eaten tapestry, where his codpiece seems
as massy as his club?

Con. All this I see; and I see that the fashion wears
out more apparel than the man. But art not
thou thyself giddy with the fashion too, that 150
thou has shifted out of thy tale into telling me
of the fashion?

Bora. Not so, neither: but know that I have to-
night wooed Margaret, the Lady Hero's gentle-
woman, by the name of Hero: she leans me
out her at mistress' chamber-window, bids me a
thousand times good night,—I tell this tale
vilely:—I should first tell thee how the prince,
Claudio and my master, planted and placed and

possessed by my master Don John, saw afar off 160
in the orchard this amiable encounter.

Con. And thought they Margaret was
Hero ?

Bora. Two of them did, the prince and Claudio ; but
the devil my master knew she was Margaret ;
and partly by his oaths, which first possessed
them, partly by the dark night, which did
deceive them, but chiefly by my villany, which
did confirm any slander that Don John had
made, away went Claudio enraged ; swore he 170
would meet her, as he was appointed, next
morning at the temple, and there, before the
whole congregation, shame her with what he
saw o'er night, and send her home again without a husband.

First Watch. We charge you, in the prince's name,
stand !

Sec. Watch. Call up the right master constable. We
have here recovered the most dangerous piece of
lechery that ever was known in the common- 180
wealth.

First Watch. And one Deformed is one of them : I
know him ; a' wears a lock.

Con. Masters, masters,—

Sec. Watch. You'll be made bring Deformed forth,
    I warrant you.

Con. Masters,—

First Watch. Never speak: we charge you let us
    obey you to go with us.

Bora. We are like to prove a goodly commodity, 190
    being taken up of these men's bills.

Con. A commodity in question, I warrant you.
    Come, we'll obey you.   [*Exeunt.*

Scene IV.

Hero's apartment.

Enter Hero, Margaret, and Ursula.

Hero. Good Ursula, wake my cousin Beatrice, and
    desire her to rise.

Urs. I will, lady.

Hero. And bid her come hither.

Urs. Well.   [*Exit.*

Marg. Troth, I think your other rabato were
    better.

Hero. No, pray thee, good Meg, I'll wear this.

Marg. By my troth's not so good; and I warrant
    your cousin will say so.   10

Hero. My cousin's a fool, and thou art another:
  I'll wear none but this.

Marg. I like the new tire within excellently, if the
  hair were a thought browner; and your gown's
  a most rare fashion, i' faith. I saw the Duchess
  of Milan's gown that they praise so.

Hero. O, that exceeds, they say.

Marg. By my troth 's but a night-gown in respect of
  yours,—cloth o' gold, and cuts, and laced with
  silver, set with pearls, down sleeves, side sleeves, 20
  and skirts, round underborne with a bluish tin-
  sel: but for a fine, quaint, graceful and excellent
  fashion, yours is worth ten on 't.

Hero. God give me joy to wear it! for my heart is
  exceeding heavy.

Marg. 'Twill be heavier soon by the weight of a
  man.

Hero. Fie upon thee! art not ashamed?

Marg. Of what, lady? of speaking honourably? Is
  not marriage honourable in a beggar? Is not 30
  your lord honourable without marriage? I think
  you would have me say, 'saving your reverence,
  a husband:' an bad thinking do not wrest true
  speaking, I'll offend nobody: is there any harm
  in 'the heavier for a husband'? None, I think,

an it be the right husband and the right wife ;
otherwise 'tis light, and not heavy : ask my
Lady Beatrice else ; here she comes.

Enter Beatrice.

Hero. Good morrow, coz.

Beat. Good morrow, sweet Hero.   40

Hero. Why, how now ? do you speak in the sick
tune ?

Beat. I am out of all other tune, methinks.

Marg. Clap 's into 'Light o' love ; ' that goes without a burden : do you sing it, and I 'll dance
it.

Beat. Ye light o' love, with your heels ! then, if your
husband have stables enough, you 'll see he shall
lack no barns.

Marg. O illegitimate construction ! I scorn that with   50
my heels.

Beat. 'Tis almost five o'clock, cousin ; 'tis time you
were ready.   By my troth, I am exceeding ill:
heigh-ho!

Marg. For a hawk, a horse, or a husband ?

Beat. For the letter that begins them all, H.

Marg. Well, an you be not turned Turk, there 's no
more sailing by the star.

72

Beat. What means the fool, trow?

Marg. Nothing I; but God send every one their   60
     heart's desire!

Hero. These gloves the count sent me; they are an
     excellent perfume.

Beat. I am stuffed, cousin; I cannot smell.

Marg. A maid, and stuffed! there's goodly catching
     of cold.

Beat. O, God help me! God help me! how long
     have you professed apprehension?

Marg. Ever since you left it. Doth not my wit be-
     come me rarely?   70

Beat. It is not seen enough, you should wear it in
     your cap. By my troth, I am sick.

Marg. Get you some of this distilled Carduus Bene-
     dictus, and lay it to your heart: it is the only
     thing for a qualm.

Hero. There thou prickest her with a thistle.

Beat. Benedictus! why Benedictus? you have some
     moral in this Benedictus.

Marg. Moral! no, by my troth, I have no moral
     meaning; I meant, plain holy-thistle. You may   80
     think perchance that I think you are in love:
     nay, by'r lady, I am not such a fool to think
     what I list; nor I list not to think what I can;

6 *f*

nor, indeed, I cannot think, if I would think my
heart out of thinking, that you are in love, or
that you will be in love, or that you can be in love.
Yet Benedick was such another, and now is he
become a man: he swore he would never marry;
and yet now, in despite of his heart, he eats his
meat without grudging: and how you may be   90
converted, I know not; but methinks you look
with your eyes as other women do.

Beat. What pace is this that thy tongue keeps?

Marg. Not a false gallop.

Re-enter Ursula.

Urs. Madam, withdraw: the prince, the count,
Signior Benedick, Don John, and all the gallants
of the town, are come to fetch you to church.

Hero. Help to dress me, good coz, good Meg, good
Ursula.   [*Exeunt.*

Scene V

Another room in Leonato's house.

Enter Leonato, with Dogberry and Verges.

Leon. What would you with me, honest neighbour?

74

Dog. Marry, sir, I would have some confidence with
    you that decerns you nearly.

Leon. Brief, I pray you ; for you see it is a busy
    time with me.

Dog. Marry, this it is, sir.

Verg. Yes, in truth it is, sir.

Leon. What is it, my good friends ?

Dog. Goodman Verges, sir, speaks a little off the   10
    matter : an old man, sir, and his wits are not
    so blunt as, God help, I would desire they were ;
    but, in faith, honest as the skin between his
    brows.

Verg. Yes, I thank God I am as honest as any man
    living that is an old man and no honester
    than I.

Dog. Comparisons are odorous : palabras, neighbour
    Verges.

Leon. Neighbours, you are tedious.   20

Dog. It pleases your worship to say so, but we are
    the poor duke's officers ; but truly, for mine
    own part, if I were as tedious as a king, I
    could find in my heart to bestow it all of your
    worship.

Leon. All thy tediousness on me, ah ?

Dog. Yea, an 't were a thousand pound more than

'tis; for I hear as good exclamation on your
worship as of any man in the city; and though I
be but a poor man, I am glad to hear it.　　　30

Verg. And so am I.

Leon. I would fain know what you have to say.

Verg. Marry, sir, our watch to-night, excepting your
worship's presence, ha' ta'en a couple of as arrant
knaves as any in Messina.

Dog. A good old man, sir; he will be talking: as
they say, When the age is in, the wit is out:
God help us! it is a world to see.　Well said,
i' faith, neighbour Verges: well, God's a good
man; an two men ride of a horse, one must ride　　40
behind.　An honest soul, i' faith, sir; by my
troth he is, as ever broke bread; but God is to
be worshipped; all men are not alike; alas,
good neighbour!

Leon. Indeed, neighbour, he comes too short of
you.

Dog. Gifts that God gives.

Leon. I must leave you.

Dog. One word, sir: our watch, sir, have indeed
comprehended two aspicious persons, and we　　50
would have them this morning examined before
your worship.

Leon. Take their examination yourself, and bring it
    me : I am now in great haste, as it may appear
    unto you.

Dog. It shall be suffigance.

Leon. Drink some wine ere you go : fare you
    well.

Enter a Messenger.

Mess. My lord, they stay for you to give your
    daughter to her husband.   60

Leon. I 'll wait upon them : I am ready.
               [Exeunt Leonato and Messenger.

Dog. Go, good partner, go, get you to Francis Sea-
    cole ; bid him bring his pen and inkhorn to the
    gaol : we are now to examination these men

Verg. And we must do it wisely.

Dog. We will spare for no wit, I warrant you ; here 's
    that shall drive some of them to a noncome :
    only get the learned writer to set down our ex-
    communication, and meet me at the gaol.   *[Exeunt.*

Act Fourth.

Scene I.

A church.

*Enter Don Pedro, Don John, Leonato, Friar Francis,
Claudio, Benedick, Hero, Beatrice, and attendants.*

Leon. Come, Friar Francis, be brief; only to the
    plain form of marriage, and you shall recount
    their particular duties afterwards.

Friar. You come hither, my lord, to marry this
    lady.

Claud. No.

Leon. To be married to her : friar, you come to
    marry her.

Friar. Lady, you come hither to be married to this
    count.   10

Hero. I do.

Friar. If either of you know any inward impediment
    why you should not be conjoined, I charge you,
    on your souls, to utter it.

Claud. Know you any, Hero ?

Hero. None, my lord.

Friar. Know you any, count?

Leon. I dare make his answer, none.

Claud. O, what men dare do! what men may do!
    what men daily do, not knowing what they   20
    do!

Bene. How now! interjections? Why, then, some
    be of laughing, as, ah, ha, he!

Claud. Stand thee by, friar. Father, by your leave:
    Will you with free and unconstrained soul
    Give me this maid, your daughter?

Leon. As freely, son, as God did give her me.

Claud. And what have I to give you back, whose worth
    May counterpoise this rich and precious gift?

D. Pedro. Nothing, unless you render her again.   30

Claud. Sweet prince, you learn me noble thankfulness.
    There, Leonato, take her back again:
    Give not this rotten orange to your friend;
    She 's but the sign and semblance of her honour.
    Behold how like a maid she blushes here!
    O, what authority and show of truth
    Can cunning sin cover itself withal!
    Comes not that blood as modest evidence
    To witness simple virtue? Would you not swear,
    All you that see her, that she were a maid,   40
    By these exterior shows? But she is none:

She knows the heat of a luxurious bed;
Her blush is guiltiness, not modesty.

Leon. What do you mean, my lord?

Claud.   Not to be married,
Not to knit my soul to an approved wanton.

Leon. Dear my lord, if you, in your own proof,
Have vanquish'd the resistance of her youth,
And made defeat of her virginity,—

Claud. I know what you would say: if I have known her,
You will say she did embrace me as a husband,   50
And so extenuate the 'forehand sin:
No, Leonato,
I never tempted her with word too large;
But, as a brother to his sister, show'd
Bashful sincerity and comely love.

Hero. And seem'd I ever otherwise to you?

Claud. Out on thee! Seeming! I will write against it
You seem to me as Dian in her orb,
As chaste as is the bud ere it be blown:
But you are more intemperate in your blood   60
Than Venus, or those pamper'd animals
That rage in savage sensuality.

Hero. Is my lord well, that he doth speak so wide?

Leon. Sweet prince, why speak not you?

D. Pedro.   What should I speak:

      I stand dishonour'd, that have gone about
      To link my dear friend to a common stale.

Leon. Are these things spoken, or do I but dream?

D. John. Sir, they are spoken, and these things are true.

Bene. This looks not like a nuptial.

Hero.   True! O God!

Claud. Leonato, stand I here?   70
      Is this the prince? is this the prince's brother?
      Is this face Hero's? are our eyes our own?

Leon. All this is so: but what of this, my lord?

Claud. Let me but move one question to your daughter;
      And, by that fatherly and kindly power
      That you have in her, bid her answer truly.

Leon. I charge thee do so, as thou art my child.

Hero. O, God defend me! how am I beset!
      What kind of catechising call you this?

Claud. To make you answer truly to your name.   80

Hero. Is it not Hero? Who can blot that name
      With any just reproach?

Claud.   Marry, that can Hero;
      Hero itself can blot out Hero's virtue.
      What man was he talk'd with you yesternight
      Out at your window betwixt twelve and one?
      Now, if you are a maid, answer to this.

Hero. I talk'd with no man at that hour, my lord.

D. Pedro. Why, then are you no maiden. Leonato,
    I am sorry you must hear: upon mine honour,
    Myself, my brother, and this grieved count   90
    Did see her, hear her, at that hour last night
    Talk with a ruffian at her chamber-window;
    Who hath indeed, most like a liberal villain,
    Confess'd the vile encounters they have had
    A thousand times in secret.

D. John. Fie, fie! they are not to be named, my lord,
    Not to be spoke of;
    There is not chastity enough in language,
    Without offence to utter them. Thus, pretty lady,
    I am sorry for thy much misgovernment.   100

Claud. O Hero, what a Hero hadst thou been,
    If half thy outward graces had been placed
    About thy thoughts and counsels of thy heart!
    But fare thee well, most foul, most fair! farewell,
    Thou pure impiety and impious purity!
    For thee I'll lock up all the gates of love,
    And on my eyelids shall conjecture hang,
    To turn all beauty into thoughts of harm,
    And never shall it more be gracious.

Leon. Hath no man's dagger here a point for me?   110
                   [Hero swoons.

Beat. Why, how now, cousin! wherefore sink you down?

D. John. Come, let us go.   These things, come thus to
      light,

    Smother her spirits up.

          [*Exeunt Don Pedro, Don John, and Claudio.*

Bene. How doth the lady?

Beat.   Dead, I think.   Help, uncle!

    Hero! why, Hero! Uncle! Signior Benedick! Friar!

Leon. O Fate! take not away thy heavy hand.

    Death is the fairest cover for her shame

    That may be wish'd for.

Beat.   How now, cousin Hero!

Friar. Have comfort, lady.

Leon. Dost thou look up?   120

Friar. Yea, wherefore should she not?

Leon. Wherefore!   Why, doth not every earthly thing

    Cry shame upon her?   Could she here deny

    The story that is printed in her blood?

    Do not live, Hero; do not ope thine eyes:

    For, did I think thou wouldst not quickly die,

    Thought I thy spirits were stronger than thy shames,

    Myself would, on the rearward of reproaches,

    Strike at thy life.   Grieved I, I had but one?

    Chid I for that at frugal nature's frame?   130

    O, one too much by thee!   Why had I one?

    Why ever wast thou lovely in my eyes?

Why had I not with charitable hand
Took up a beggar's issue at my gates,
Who smirched thus and mired with infamy,
I might have said, ' No part of it is mine ;
This shame derives itself from unknown loins ' ?
But mine, and mine I loved, and mine I praised,
And mine that I was proud on, mine so much
That I myself was to myself not mine,   140
Valuing of her,—why, she, O, she is fallen
Into a pit of ink, that the wide sea
Hath drops too few to wash her clean again,
And salt too little which may season give
To her foul-tainted flesh !

Bene.   Sir, sir, be patient.
For my part, I am so attired in wonder,
I know not what to say.

Beat. O, on my soul, my cousin is belied !

Bene. Lady, were you her bedfellow last night ?

Beat. No, truly, not ; although, until last night,   150
I have this twelvemonth been her bedfellow.

Leon. Confirm'd, confirm'd !　O, that is stronger made
Which was before barr'd up with ribs of iron !
Would the two princes lie, and Claudio lie,
Who loved her so, that, speaking of her foulness,
Wash'd it with tears ? Hence from her ! let her die.

Friar. Hear me a little ;
    For I have only been silent so long,
    And given way unto this course of fortune,
    By noting of the lady : I have mark'd   160
    A thousand blushing apparitions
    To start into her face ; a thousand innocent shames
    In angel whiteness beat away those blushes ;
    And in her eye there hath appear'd a fire,
    To burn the errors that these princes hold
    Against her maiden truth.   Call me a fool ;
    Trust not my reading nor my observations,
    Which with experimental seal doth warrant
    The tenour of my book ; trust not my age,
    My reverence, calling, nor divinity,   170
    If this sweet lady lie not guiltless here
    Under some biting error.

Leon.   Friar, it cannot be.
    Thou seest that all the grace that she hath left
    Is that she will not add to her damnation
    A sin of perjury ; she not denies it :
    Why seek'st thou, then, to cover with excuse
    That which appears in proper nakedness ?

Friar. Lady, what man is he you are accused of ?

Hero. They know that do accuse me ; I know none :
    If I know more of any man alive   180

    Than that which maiden modesty doth warrant,
    Let all my sins lack mercy! O my father,
    Prove you that any man with me conversed
    At hours unmeet, or that I yesternight
    Maintain'd the change of words with any creature,
    Refuse me, hate me, torture me to death!

Friar. There is some strange misprision in the princes.

Bene. Two of them have the very bent of honour;
    And if their wisdoms be misled in this,
    The practice of it lives in John the bastard,   190
    Whose spirits toil in frame of villanies.

Leon. I know not.   If they speak but truth of her,
    These hands shall tear her; if they wrong her honour,
    The proudest of them shall well hear of it.
    Time hath not yet so dried this blood of mine,
    Nor age so eat up my invention,
    Nor fortune made such havoc of my means,
    Nor my bad life reft me so much of friends,
    But they shall find, awaked in such a kind,
    Both strength of limb and policy of mind,   200
    Ability in means and choice of friends,
    To quit me of them thoroughly.

Friar.   Pause awhile,
    And let my counsel sway you in this case.
    Your daughter here the princes left for dead:

    Let her awhile be secretly kept in,

    And publish it that she is dead indeed;

    Maintain a mourning ostentation,

    And on your family's old monument

    Hang mournful epitaphs, and do all rites

    That appertain unto a burial.   210

Leon. What shall become of this? what will this do?

Friar. Marry, this, well carried, shall on her behalf

    Change slander to remorse; that is some good:

    But not for that dream I on this strange course,

    But on this travail look for greater birth.

    She dying, as it must be so maintain'd,

    Upon the instant that she was accused,

    Shall be lamented, pitied, and excused

    Of every hearer: for it so falls out,

    That what we have we prize not to the worth 220

    Whiles we enjoy it; but being lack'd and lost,

    Why, then we rack the value, then we find

    The virtue that possession would not show us

    Whiles it was ours.   So will it fare with Claudio:

    When he shall hear she died upon his words,

    The idea of her life shall sweetly creep

    Into his study of imagination;

    And every lovely organ of her life

    Shall come apparell'd in more precious habit,

More moving-delicate and full of life,　　　　230
Into the eye and prospect of his soul,
Than when she lived indeed ; then shall he mourn,
If ever love had interest in his liver,
And wish he had not so accused her,
No, though he thought his accusation true.
Let this be so, and doubt not but success
Will fashion the event in better shape
Than I can lay it down in likelihood.
But if all aim but this be levell'd false,
The supposition of the lady's death　　　　240
Will quench the wonder of her infamy :
And if it sort not well, you may conceal her,
As best befits her wounded reputation,
In some reclusive and religious life,
Out of all eyes, tongues, minds, and injuries.

Bene. Signior Leonato, let the friar advise you :
And though you know my inwardness and love
Is very much unto the prince and Claudio,
Yet, by mine honour, I will deal in this
As secretly and justly as your soul　　　　250
Should with your body.

Leon.　　　　　　　　Being that I flow in grief,
The smallest twine may lead me.

Friar. 'Tis well consented : presently away ;

      For to strange sores strangely they strain the cure.
    Come, lady, die to live : this wedding-day
      Perhaps is but prolong'd : have patience and en-
          dure.   [*Exeunt all but Benedick and Beatrice.*

Bene. Lady Beatrice, have you wept all this while?

Beat. Yea, and I will weep a while longer.

Bene. I will not desire that.

Beat. You have no reason ; I do it freely.   260

Bene. Surely I do believe your fair cousin is
    wronged.

Beat. Ah, how much might the man deserve of me
    that would right her!

Bene. Is there any way to show such friendship?

Beat. A very even way, but no such friend.

Bene. May a man do it?

Beat. It is a man's office, but not yours.

Bene. I do love nothing in the world so well as you :
    is not that strange?   270

Beat. As strange as the thing I know not.   It were
    as possible for me to say I loved nothing so well
    as you : but believe me not ; and yet I lie not ;
    I confess nothing, nor I deny nothing.   I am
    sorry for my cousin.

Bene. By my sword, Beatrice, thou lovest me.

Beat. Do not swear, and eat it.

Bene. I will swear by it that you love me; and I will
     make him eat it that says I love not you.

Beat. Will you not eat your word?   280

Bene. With no sauce that can be devised to it. I
     protest I love thee.

Beat. Why, then, God forgive me!

Bene. What offence, sweet Beatrice?

Beat. You have stayed me in a happy hour: I was
     about to protest I loved you.

Bene. And do it with all thy heart.

Beat. I love you with so much of my heart, that
     none is left to protest.

Bene. Come, bid me do any thing for thee.   290

Beat. Kill Claudio.

Bene. Ha! not for the wide world.

Beat. You kill me to deny it. Farewell.

Bene. Tarry, sweet Beatrice.

Beat. I am gone, though I am here: there is no love
     in you: nay, I pray you, let me go.

Bene. Beatrice,—

Beat. In faith, I will go.

Bene. We'll be friends first.

Beat. You dare easier be friends with me than fight 300
     with mine enemy.

Bene. Is Claudio thine enemy?

Beat. Is he not approved in the height a villain, that
     hath slandered, scorned, dishonoured my kins-
     woman? O that I were a man! What, bear
     her in hand until they come to take hands; and
     then, with public accusation, uncovered slander,
     unmitigated rancour,—O God, that I were a
     man! I would eat his heart in the market-place.

Bene. Hear me, Beatrice,—   310

Beat. Talk with a man out at a window! A proper
     saying!

Bene. Nay, but, Beatrice,—

Beat. Sweet Hero! She is wronged, she is slandered,
     she is undone.

Bene. Beat—

Beat. Princes and counties! Surely, a princely testi-
     mony, a goodly count, Count Comfect; a sweet
     gallant, surely! O that I were a man for his
     sake! or that I had any friend would be a man 320
     for my sake! But manhood is melted into
     courtesies, valour into compliment, and men are
     only turned into tongue, and trim ones too: he
     is now as valiant as Hercules that only tells a lie,
     and swears it. I cannot be a man with wishing,
     therefore I will die a woman with grieving.

Bene. Tarry, good Beatrice. By this hand, I love
     thee.   91

Beat. Use it for my love some other way than
　　swearing by it.　　　　　　　　　　　330
Bene. Think you in your soul the Count Claudio
　　hath wronged Hero?
Beat. Yea, as sure as I have a thought or a
　　soul.
Bene. Enough, I am engaged; I will challenge him.
　　I will kiss your hand, and so I leave you.　By
　　this hand, Claudio shall render me a dear
　　account.　As you hear of me, so think of
　　me.　Go, comfort your cousin: I must say
　　she is dead: and so, farewell.　　　[*Exeunt.* 340

Scene II.

A prison.

*Enter Dogberry, Verges, and Sexton, in gowns; and
the Watch, with Conrade and Borachio.*

Dog. Is our whole dissembly appeared?
Verg. O, a stool and a cushion for the sexton.
Sex. Which be the malefactors?
Dog. Marry, that am I and my partner.
Verg. Nay, that's certain; we have the exhibition
　　to examine.

Sex. But which are the offenders that are to be examined? let them come before master constable.

Dog. Yea, marry, let them come before me. What   10
is your name, friend?

Bora. Borachio.

Dog. Pray, write down, Borachio. Yours,
sirrah?

Con. I am a gentleman, sir, and my name is
Conrade.

Dog. Write down, master gentleman Conrade.
Masters, do you serve God?

Con.
Bora. } Yea, sir, we hope.

Dog. Write down, that they hope they serve God: 20
and write God first; for God defend but God
should go before such villains! Masters, it is
proved already that you are little better than
false knaves; and it will go near to be thought
so shortly. How answer you for yourselves?

Con. Marry, sir, we say we are none.

Dog. A marvellous witty fellow, I assure you; but
I will go about with him. Come you hither,
sirrah; a word in your ear: sir, I say to you,
it is thought you are false knaves.   30

Bora. Sir, I say to you we are none.

Dog. Well, stand aside. 'Fore God, they are both
    in a tale. Have you writ down, that they are
    none?

Sex. Master Constable, you go not the way to
    examine: you must call forth the watch that are
    their accusers.

Dog. Yea, marry, that's the eftest way. Let the
    watch come forth. Masters, I charge you, in
    the prince's name, accuse these men.   40

First Watch. This man said, sir, that Don John, the
    prince's brother, was a villain.

Dog. Write down, Prince John a villain. Why, this
    is flat perjury, to call a prince's brother villain.

Bora. Master Constable,—

Dog. Pray thee, fellow, peace: I do not like thy
    look, I promise thee.

Sex. What heard you him say else?

Sec. Watch. Marry, that he had received a thousand
    ducats of Don John for accusing the Lady   50
    Hero wrongfully.

Dog. Flat burglary as ever was committed.

Verg. Yea, by mass, that it is.

Sex. What else, fellow?

First Watch. And that Count Claudio did mean, upon

his words, to disgrace Hero before the whole
assembly, and not marry her.

Dog. O villain! thou wilt be condemned into ever-
lasting redemption for this.

Sex. What else?   60

Watch. This is all.

Sex. And this is more, masters, than you can deny.
Prince John is this morning secretly stolen away;
Hero was in this manner accused, in this very
manner refused, and upon the grief of this sud-
denly died. Master constable, let these men be
bound, and brought to Leonato's: I will go
before and show him their examination. [*Exit.*

Dog. Come, let them be opinioned.

Verg. Let them be in the hands—   70

Con. Off, coxcomb!

Dog. God's my life, where's the sexton? let him
write down, the prince's officer, coxcomb.
Come, bind them. Thou naughty varlet!

Con. Away! you are an ass, you are an ass.

Dog. Dost thou not suspect my place? dost thou not
suspect my years? O that he were here to write
me down an ass! But, masters, remember that
I am an ass; though it be not written down,
yet forget not that I am an ass. No, thou vil-   80

lain, thou art full of piety, as shall be proved
upon thee by good witness. I am a wise fellow;
and, which is more, an officer; and, which is
more, a householder; and, which is more, as
pretty a piece of flesh as any is in Messina; and
one that knows the law, go to; and a rich fellow
enough, go to; and a fellow that hath had losses;
and one that hath two gowns, and every thing
handsome about him. Bring him away. O
that I had been writ down an ass!   [*Exeunt.* 90

Act Fifth.

Scene I.

Before Leonato's house.

Enter Leonato and Antonio.

Ant. If you go on thus, you will kill yourself;
And 'tis not wisdom thus to second grief
Against yourself.

Leon.   I pray thee, cease thy counsel,
Which falls into mine ears as profitless
As water in a sieve: give not me counsel;

Nor let no comforter delight mine ear
But such a one whose wrongs do suit with mine.
Bring me a father that so loved his child,
Whose joy of her is overwhelm'd like mine,
And bid him speak of patience ;   10
Measure his woe the length and breadth of mine,
And let it answer every strain for strain,
As thus for thus, and such a grief for such,
In every lineament, branch, shape, and form :
If such a one will smile, and stroke his beard,
Bid sorrow wag, cry 'hem !' when he should groan,
Patch grief with proverbs, make misfortune drunk
With candle-wasters ; bring him yet to me,
And I of him will gather patience.
But there is no such man : for, brother, men   20
Can counsel and speak comfort to that grief
Which they themselves not feel ; but, tasting it,
Their counsel turns to passion, which before
Would give preceptial medicine to rage,
Fetter strong madness in a silken thread,
Charm ache with air, and agony with words :
No, no ; 'tis all men's office to speak patience
To those that wring under the load of sorrow,
But no man's virtue nor sufficiency,
To be so moral when he shall endure   30

The like himself.   Therefore give me no counsel:
My griefs cry louder than advertisement.

Ant. Therein do men from children nothing differ.

Leon. I pray thee, peace.   I will be flesh and blood;
For there was never yet philosopher
That could endure the toothache patiently,
However they have writ the style of gods,
And made a push at chance and sufferance.

Ant. Yet bend not all the harm upon yourself;
Make those that do offend you suffer too.   40

Leon. There thou speak'st reason : nay, I will do so.
My soul doth tell me Hero is belied;
And that shall Claudio know; so shall the prince,
And all of them that thus dishonour her.

Ant. Here comes the prince and Claudio hastily.

Enter Don Pedro and Claudio.

D. Pedro. Good den, good den.

Claud.   Good day to both of you.

Leon. Hear you, my lords,—

D. Pedro.   We have some haste, Leonato.

Leon. Some haste, my lord! well, fare you well, my lord:
Are you so hasty now? well, all is one.

D. Pedro. Nay, do not quarrel with us, good old man. 50

Ant. If he could right himself with quarrelling,
    Some of us would lie low.

Claud.   Who wrongs him :

Leon. Marry, thou dost wrong me, thou dissembler, thou :—
    Nay, never lay thy hand upon thy sword ;
    I fear thee not.

Claud.   Marry, beshrew my hand,
    If it should give your age such cause of fear :
    In faith, my hand meant nothing to my sword.

Leon. Tush, tush, man ; never fleer and jest **at me** :
    I speak not like a dotard nor a fool,
    As, under privilege of age, to brag   60
    What I have done being young, or what would do,
    Were I not old.   Know, Claudio, to thy head,
    Thou hast so wrong'd mine innocent child and me,
    That I am forced to lay my reverence by,
    And, with grey hairs and bruise of many days,
    Do challenge thee to trial of a man.
    I say thou hast belied mine innocent child ;
    Thy slander hath gone through and through her heart,
    And she lies buried with her ancestors ;
    O, in a tomb where never scandal slept,   70
    Save this of hers, framed by thy villany !

Claud. My villany ?

Leon.   Thine, Claudio ; thine, I say.

D. Pedro. You say not right, old man.

Leon.   My lord, my lord,
  I 'll prove it on his body, if he dare,
  Despite his nice fence and his active practice,
  His May of youth and bloom of lustihood.

Claud. Away! I will not have to do with you.

Leon. Canst thou so daff me? Thou hast kill'd my child:
  If thou kill'st me, boy, thou shalt kill a man.

Ant. He shall kill two of us, and men indeed: 80
  But that 's no matter; let him kill one first;
  Win me and wear me; let him answer me.
  Come, follow me, boy; come, sir boy, come, follow
   me:
  Sir boy, I 'll whip you from your foining fence;
  Nay, as I am a gentleman, I will.

Leon. Brother,—

Ant. Content yourself. God knows I loved my niece;
  And she is dead, slander'd to death by villains,
  That dare as well answer a man indeed
  As I dare take a serpent by the tongue: 90
  Boys, apes, braggarts, Jacks, milksops!

Leon.   Brother Antony,—

Ant. Hold you content. What, man! I know them, yea,
  And what they weigh, even to the utmost scruple,—
  Scambling, out-facing, fashion-monging boys,

That lie, and cog, and flout, deprave, and slander,
Go antiquely, and show outward hideousness,
And speak off half a dozen dangerous words,
How they might hurt their enemies, if they durst;
And this is all.

Leon. But, brother Antony,—

Ant.   Come, 'tis no matter: 100
    Do not you meddle; let me deal in this.

D. Pedro. Gentlemen both, we will not wake your patience.
    My heart is sorry for your daughter's death:
    But, on my honour, she was charged with nothing
    But what was true, and very full of proof.

Leon. My lord, my lord,—

D. Pedro. I will not hear you.

Leon. No? Come, brother; away! I will be heard.

Ant. And shall, or some of us will smart for it.

                     [*Exeunt Leonato and Antonio.*

D. Pedro. See, see; here comes the man we went to seek.

          Enter Benedick.

Claud. Now, signior, what news?   111

Bene. Good day, my lord.

D. Pedro. Welcome, signior: you are almost come
    to part almost a fray.

Claud. We had like to have had our two noses
    snapped off with two old men without teeth.

D. Pedro. Leonato and his brother. What thinkest
    thou? Had we fought, I doubt we should
    have been too young for them.

Bene. In a false quarrel there is no true valour.   I 120
    came to seek you both.

Claud. We have been up and down to seek thee;
    for we are high-proof melancholy, and would fain
    have it beaten away. Wilt thou use thy wit?

Bene. It is in my scabbard: shall I draw it?

D. Pedro. Dost thou wear thy wit by thy side?

Claud. Never any did so, though very many have
    been beside their wit. I will bid thee draw, as
    we do the minstrels; draw, to pleasure us.

D. Pedro. As I am an honest man, he looks pale. 130
    Art thou sick, or angry?

Claud. What, courage, man! What though care
    killed a cat, thou hast mettle enough in thee to
    kill care.

Bene. Sir, I shall meet your wit in the career, an
    you charge it against me. I pray you choose
    another subject.

Claud. Nay, then, give him another staff: this last
    was broke cross.

D. Pedro. By this light, he changes more and more : 140
    I think he be angry indeed.

Claud. If he be, he knows how to turn his
    girdle.

Bene. Shall I speak a word in your ear ?

Claud. God bless me from a challenge !

Bene. [*Aside to Claudio*] You are a villain ; I jest
    not : I will make it good how you dare, with
    what you dare, and when you dare. Do me
    right, or I will protest your cowardice. You
    have killed a sweet lady, and her death shall 150
    fall heavy on you. Let me hear from you.

Claud. Well, I will meet you, so I may have good
    cheer.

D. Pedro. What, a feast, a feast ?

Claud. I' faith, I thank him ; he hath bid me to a
    calf's-head and a capon ; the which if I do not
    carve most curiously, say my knife 's naught.
    Shall I not find a woodcock too ?

Bene. Sir, your wit ambles well ; it goes easily.

D. Pedro. I 'll tell thee how Beatrice praised thy wit 160
    the other day. I said, thou hadst a fine wit :
    'True,' said she, 'a fine little one.' 'No,' said
    I, 'a great wit :' 'Right,' says she, 'a great gross
    one.' 'Nay,' said I, 'a good wit :' 'Just,' said

she, 'it hurts nobody.' 'Nay,' said I, 'the
gentleman is wise:' 'Certain,' said she, 'a wise
gentleman.' 'Nay,' said I, 'he hath the tongues:'
'That I believe,' said she, 'for he swore a thing
to me on Monday night, which he forswore
on Tuesday morning; there's a double tongue;   170
there's two tongues.' Thus did she, an hour
together, trans-shape thy particular virtues: yet
at last she concluded with a sigh, thou wast the
properest man in Italy.

Claud. For the which she wept heartily, and said she
cared not.

D. Pedro. Yea, that she did; but yet, for all that,
an if she did not hate him deadly, she would
love him dearly: the old man's daughter told
us all.   180

Claud. All, all; and, moreover, God saw him when
he was hid in the garden.

D. Pedro. But when shall we set the savage bull's
horns on the sensible Benedick's head?

Claud. Yea, and text underneath, 'Here dwells
Benedick the married man'?

Bene. Fare you well, boy: you know my mind. I
will leave you now to your gossip-like humour:
you break jests as braggarts do their blades,

which, God be thanked, hurt not. My lord, 190
for your many courtesies I thank you: I must
discontinue your company: your brother the
bastard is fled from Messina: you have among
you killed a sweet and innocent lady. For my
Lord Lackbeard there, he and I shall meet:
and till then peace be with him. [*Exit.*

D. Pedro. He is in earnest.

Claud. In most profound earnest; and, I'll warrant
 you, for the love of Beatrice.

D. Pedro. And hath challenged thee.   200

Claud. Most sincerely.

D. Pedro. What a pretty thing man is when he goes
 in his doublet and hose, and leaves off his
 wit!

Claud. He is then a giant to an ape: but then is an
 ape a doctor to such a man.

D. Pedro. But, soft you, let me be: pluck up,
 my heart, and be sad. Did he not say, my
 brother was fled?

*Enter Dogberry, Verges, and the Watch, with Conrade
and Borachio.*

Dog. Come, you, sir: if justice cannot tame you, she 210
shall ne'er weigh more reasons in her balance:

6 *h*

nay, an you be a cursing hypocrite once, you
must be looked to.

D. Pedro. How now? two of my brother's men
    bound!   Borachio one!

Claud. Hearken after their offence, my lord.

D. Pedro. Officers, what offence have these men
    done?

Dog. Marry, sir, they have committed false report;
    moreover, they have spoken untruths; secon- 220
    darily, they are slanders; sixth and lastly, they
    have belied a lady; thirdly, they have verified
    unjust things; and, to conclude, they are lying
    knaves.

D. Pedro. First, I ask thee what they have done;
    thirdly, I ask thee what's their offence; sixth
    and lastly, why they are committed; and, to
    conclude, what you lay to their charge.

Claud. Rightly reasoned, and in his own division;
    and, by my troth, there's one meaning well 230
    suited.

D. Pedro. Who have you offended, masters, that
    you are thus bound to your answer? this learned
    constable is too cunning to be understood:
    what's your offence?

Bora. Sweet prince, let me go no farther to mine

answer: do you hear me, and let this count kill
me. I have deceived even your very eyes:
what your wisdoms could not discover, these
shallow fools have brought to light; who, in 240
the night, overheard me confessing to this man,
how Don John your brother incensed me to
slander the Lady Hero; how you were brought
into the orchard, and saw me court Margaret in
Hero's garments: how you disgraced her, when
you should marry her: my villany they have
upon record; which I had rather seal with my
death than repeat over to my shame. The lady
is dead upon mine and my master's false accusation; and, briefly, I desire nothing but the 250
reward of a villain.

D. Pedro. Runs not this speech like iron through
      your blood?

Claud. I have drunk poison whiles he utter'd it.

D. Pedro. But did my brother set thee on to this?

Bora. Yea, and paid me richly for the practice of
      it.

D. Pedro. He is composed and framed of treachery:
      And fled he is upon this villany.

Claud. Sweet Hero! now thy image doth appear
      In the rare semblance that I loved it first.   260

Dog. **Come**, bring away the plaintiffs: by this time
our sexton hath reformed Signior Leonato of
the matter: and, masters, do not forget to
specify, when time and place shall serve, that
I am an ass.

Verg. Here, here comes master Signior Leonato,
and the sexton too.

Re-enter Leonato and Antonio, with the Sexton.

Leon. Which is the villain? let me see his eyes,
That, when I note another man like him,   270
I may avoid him: which of these is he?

Bora. If you would know your wronger, look on me.

Leon. Art thou the slave that with thy breath hast kill'd
Mine innocent child?

Bora.   Yea, even I alone.

Leon. No, not so, villain; thou beliest thyself:
Here stand a pair of honourable men;
A third is fled, that had a hand in it.
I thank you, princes, for my daughter's death:
Record it with your high and worthy deeds:
'Twas bravely done, if you bethink you of it.

Claud. I know not how to pray your patience;   280
Yet I must speak.   Choose your revenge yourself;
Impose me to what penance your invention

Can lay upon my sin : yet sinn'd I not
But in mistaking.

D. Pedro.   By my soul, nor I :
And yet, to satisfy this good old man,
I would bend under any heavy weight
That he 'll enjoin me to.

Leon. I cannot bid you bid my daughter live ;
That were impossible : but, I pray you both,
Possess the people in Messina here   290
How innocent she died ; and if your love
Can labour aught in sad invention,
Hang her an epitaph upon her tomb,
And sing it to her bones, sing it to-night :
To-morrow morning come you to my house ;
And since you could not be my son-in-law,
Be yet my nephew : my brother hath a daughter,
Almost the copy of my child that 's dead,
And she alone is heir to both of us :
Give her the right you should have given her cousin,
And so dies my revenge.

Claud.   O noble sir,   301
Your over-kindness doth wring tears from me !
I do embrace your offer ; and dispose
For henceforth of poor Claudio.

Leon. To-morrow, then, I will expect your coming ;

To-night I take my leave.   This naughty man
Shall face to face be brought to Margaret,
Who I believe was pack'd in all this wrong,
Hired to it by your brother.

Bora.   No, by my soul, she was not;
Nor knew not what she did when she spoke to me;
But always hath been just and virtuous   311
In any thing that I do know by her.

Dog. Moreover, sir, which indeed is not under white
and black, this plaintiff here, the offender, did call
me ass: I beseech you, let it be remembered
in his punishment.   And also, the watch heard
them talk of one Deformed: they say he wears
a key in his ear, and a lock hanging by it; and
borrows money in God's name, the which he hath
used so long and never paid, that now men grow   320
hard-hearted, and will lend nothing for God's
sake: pray you, examine him upon that point.

Leon. I thank thee for thy care and honest pains.

Dog. Your worship speaks like a most thankful and
reverend youth; and I praise God for you.

Leon. There's for thy pains.

Dog. God save the foundation!

Leon. Go, I discharge thee of thy prisoner, and I
thank thee.

Dog. I leave an arrant knave with your worship; 330
  which I beseech your worship to correct yourself, for the example of others.   God keep your
  worship!   I wish your worship well; God restore you to health!   I humbly give you leave
  to depart; and if a merry meeting may be wished,
  God prohibit it!   Come, neighbour.

[Exeunt Dogberry and Verges.

Leon. Until to-morrow morning, lords, farewell.

Ant. Farewell, my lords: we look for you to-morrow.

D. Pedro. We will not fail.

Claud.   To-night I'll mourn with Hero.

Leon. [*To the Watch*] Bring you these fellows on.
  We'll talk with Margaret,   340
  How her acquaintance grew with this lewd fellow.

[Exeunt, severally.

Scene II.

Leonato's garden.

Enter Benedick and Margaret, meeting.

Bene. Pray thee, sweet Mistress Margaret, deserve
  well at my hands by helping me to the speech
  of Beatrice.

Marg. Will you, then, write me a sonnet in praise
  of my beauty?   111

Bene. In so high a style, Margaret, that no man living shall come over it ; for, in most comely truth, thou deservest it.

Marg. To have no man come over me ! why, shall I always keep below stairs ?   10

Bene. Thy wit is as quick as the greyhound's mouth ; it catches.

Marg. And yours as blunt as the fencer's foils, which hit, but hurt not.

Bene. A most manly wit, Margaret ; it will not hurt a woman : and so, I pray thee, call Beatrice : I give thee the bucklers.

Marg. Give us the swords ; we have bucklers of our own.

Bene. If you use them, Margaret, you must put in   20 the pikes with a vice ; and they are dangerous weapons for maids.

Marg. Well, I will call Beatrice to you, who I think hath legs.

Bene. And therefore will come.   [*Exit Margaret.*

[*Sings*]   The god of love,
          That sits above,
     And knows me, and knows me,
          How pitiful I deserve,—

I mean in singing; but in loving, Leander the good 30
swimmer, Troilus the first employer of pandars,
and a whole bookful of these quondam carpet-
mongers, whose names yet run smoothly in the even
road of a blank verse, why, they were never so
truly turned over and over as my poor self in love.
Marry, I cannot show it in rhyme; I have tried:
I can find out no rhyme to 'lady' but 'baby,'
an innocent rhyme; for 'scorn,' 'horn,' a hard
rhyme; for 'school,' 'fool,' a babbling rhyme;
very ominous endings: no, I was not born under a 40
rhyming planet, nor I cannot woo in festival terms.

Enter Beatrice.

Sweet Beatrice, wouldst thou come when I
called thee?

Beat. Yea, signior, and depart when you bid me.

Bene. O, stay but till then!

Beat. 'Then' is spoken; fare you well now: and
yet, ere I go, let me go with that I came; which
is, with knowing what hath passed between you
and Claudio.

Bene. Only foul words; and thereupon I will kiss 50
thee.

Beat. Foul words is but foul wind, and foul wind is

but foul breath, and foul breath is noisome;
therefore I will depart unkissed.

Bene. Thou hast frighted the word out of his right
sense, so forcible is thy wit. But I must tell
thee plainly, Claudio undergoes my challenge;
and either I must shortly hear from him, or I
will subscribe him a coward. And, I pray thee
now, tell me for which of my bad parts didst 60
thou first fall in love with me?

Beat. For them all together; which maintained so
politic a state of evil, that they will not admit
any good part to intermingle with them. But
for which of my good parts did you first suffer
love for me?

Bene. Suffer love,—a good epithet! I do suffer love
indeed, for I love thee against my will.

Beat. In spite of your heart, I think; alas, poor
heart! If you spite it for my sake, I will spite 70
it for yours; for I will never love that which
my friend hates.

Bene. Thou and I are too wise to woo peace-
ably.

Beat. It appears not in this confession: there's not
one wise man among twenty that will praise
himself.

Bene. An old, an old instance, Beatrice, that lived
    in the time of good neighbours. If a man do
    not erect in this age his own tomb ere he dies,   80
    he shall live no longer in monument than the
    bell rings and the widow weeps.

Beat. And how long is that, think you?

Bene. Question : why, an hour in clamour, and a
    quarter in rheum : therefore is it most expedient
    for the wise, if Don Worm, his conscience, find
    no impediment to the contrary, to be the trumpet
    of his own virtues, as I am to myself.   So much
    for praising myself, who, I myself will bear wit-
    ness, is praiseworthy : and now tell me, how   90
    doth your cousin ?

Beat. Very ill.

Bene. And how do you?

Beat. Very ill too.

Bene. Serve God, love me, and mend.   There will
    I leave you too, for here comes one in haste.

Enter Ursula.

Urs. Madam, you must come to your uncle.   Yon-
    der's old coil at home : it is proved my Lady
    Hero hath been falsely accused, the prince and
    Claudio mightily abused ; and Don John is the   100

author of all, who is fled and gone. Will you
come presently?

Beat. Will you go hear this news, signior?

Bene. I will live in thy heart, die in thy lap, and be
buried in thy eyes; and moreover I will go with
thee to thy uncle's. *[Exeunt.*

Scene III.

A church.

Enter Don Pedro, Claudio, and three or four with tapers.

Claud. Is this the monument of Leonato?

A Lord. It is, my lord.

Claud. [*Reading out of a scroll*]

> Done to death by slanderous tongues
>   Was the Hero that here lies:
> Death, in guerdon of her wrongs,
>   Gives her fame which never dies.
> So the life that died with shame
> Lives in death with glorious fame.

> Hang thou there upon the tomb,
> Praising her when I am dumb.

Now, music, sound, and sing your solemn hymn. 10

SONG.

Pardon, goddess of the night,
Those that slew thy virgin knight;
For the which, with songs of woe,
Round about her tomb they go.
    Midnight, assist our moan;
    Help us to sigh and groan,
        Heavily, heavily:
Graves, yawn, and yield your dead,
Till death be uttered,   20
        Heavily, heavily.

Claud. Now, unto thy bones good night!
    Yearly will I do this rite.
D. Pedro. Good morrow, masters; put your torches out:
    The wolves have prey'd; and look, the gentle day,
Before the wheels of Phœbus, round about
Dapples the drowsy east with spots of grey.
Thanks to you all, and leave us: fare you well.
Claud. Good morrow, masters: each his several way.
D. Pedro. Come, let us hence, and put on other weeds;
    And then to Leonato's we will go.   31
Claud. And Hymen now with luckier issue speed's
    Than this for whom we render'd up this woe.
                      [Exeunt.

Scene IV.

A room in Leonato's house.

Enter Leonato, Antonio, Benedick, Beatrice, Margaret,
Ursula, Friar Francis, and Hero.

Friar. Did I not tell you she was innocent?
Leon. So are the prince and Claudio, who accused her
　　Upon the error that you heard debated:
　　But Margaret was in some fault for this,
　　Although against her will, as it appears
　　In the true course of all the question.
Ant. Well, I am glad that all things sort so well.
Bene. And so am I, being else by faith enforced
　　To call young Claudio to a reckoning for it.
Leon. Well, daughter, and you gentlewomen all,
　　Withdraw into a chamber by yourselves,
　　And when I send for you, come hither mask'd.
　　　　　　　　　　　　　　　　[Exeunt Ladies.
　　The prince and Claudio promised by this hour
　　To visit me.　You know your office, brother:
　　You must be father to your brother's daughter,
　　And give her to young Claudio.
Ant. Which I will do with confirm'd countenance.

Bene. Friar, I must entreat your pains, I think

Friar. To do what, signior?

Bene. To bind me, or undo me; one of them.   20

    Signior Leonato, truth it is, good signior,

    Your niece regards me with an eye of favour.

Leon. That eye my daughter lent her: 'tis most true.

Bene. And I do with an eye of love requite her.

Leon. The sight whereof I think you had from me,

    From Claudio, and the prince: but what's your will?

Bene. Your answer, sir, is enigmatical:

    But, for my will, my will is, your good will

    May stand with ours, this day to be conjoin'd

    In the state of honourable marriage: 30

    In which, good friar, I shall desire your help.

Leon. My heart is with your liking

Friar.   And my help.

    Here comes the prince and Claudio.

Enter Don Pedro and Claudio, and two or three others.

D. Pedro. Good morrow to this fair assembly.

Leon. Good morrow, prince; good morrow, Claudio:

    We here attend you.   Are you yet determined

    To-day to marry with my brother's daughter?

Claud. I'll hold my mind, were she an Ethiope.

Leon. Call her forth, brother; here's the friar ready.

                             [*Exit Antonio.*

D. Pedro. Good morrow, Benedick. Why, what's the matter,   40

    That you have such a February face,

    So full of frost, of storm, and cloudiness?

Claud. I think he thinks upon the savage bull.

    Tush, fear not, man; we'll tip thy horns with gold,

    And all Europa shall rejoice at thee;

    As once Europa did at lusty Jove,

    When he would play the noble beast in love.

Bene. Bull Jove, sir, had an amiable low;

    And some such strange bull leap'd your father's cow,

    And got a calf in that same noble feat   50

    Much like to you, for you have just his bleat.

Claud. For this I owe you: here comes other reckonings.

Re-enter Antonio, with the Ladies masked.

    Which is the lady I must seize upon?

Ant. This same is she, and I do give you her.

Claud. Why, then she's mine. Sweet, let me see your face.

Leon. No, that you shall not, till you take her hand

    Before this friar, and swear to marry her.

Claud. Give me your hand: before this holy friar,

     I am your husband, if you like of me.

Hero. And when I lived, I was your other wife :   60

                          [*Unmasking.*

     And when you loved, you were my other husband.

Claud. Another Hero !

Hero.   Nothing certainer :

     One Hero died defiled ; but I do live

     And surely as I live, I am a maid.

D. Pedro. The former Hero ! Hero that is dead !

Leon. She died, my lord, but whiles her slander lived.

Friar. All this amazement can I qualify :

     When after that the holy rites are ended,

     I 'll tell you largely of fair Hero's death :

     Meantime let wonder seem familiar,   70

     And to the chapel let us presently.

Bene. Soft and fair, friar. Which is Beatrice ?

Beat. [*Unmasking*] I answer to that name. What is
       your will ?

Bene. Do not you love me ?

Beat.   Why, no ; no more than reason.

Bene. Why, then your uncle, and the prince, and Claudio
     Have been deceived ; they swore you did.

Beat. Do not you love me ?

Bene.   Troth, no ; no more than reason.

Beat. Why, then my cousin, Margaret, and Ursula

Are much deceived; for they did swear you did.

Bene. They swore that you were almost sick for me. 80

Beat. They swore that you were well-nigh dead for me.

Bene. 'Tis no such matter. Then you do not love me?

Beat. No, truly, but in friendly recompense.

Leon. Come, cousin, I am sure you love the gentleman.

Claud. And I'll be sworn upon 't that he loves her;
   For here's a paper, written in his hand,
   A halting sonnet of his own pure brain,
   Fashion'd to Beatrice.

Hero.   And here's another,
   Writ in my cousin's hand, stolen from her pocket,
   Containing her affection unto Benedick. 90

Bene. A miracle! here's our own hands against our
   hearts. Come, I will have thee; but, by this
   light, I take thee for pity.

Beat. I would not deny you; but, by this good day,
   I yield upon great persuasion; and partly to save
   your life, for I was told you were in a
   consumption.

Bene. Peace! I will stop your mouth.   [*Kissing her.*

D. Pedro. How dost thou, Benedick, the married
   man? 100

Bene. I'll tell thee what, prince; a college of wit-
   crackers cannot flout me out of my humour.

Dost thou think I care for a satire or an epigram?
No: if a man will be beaten with brains, a' shall
wear nothing handsome about him. In brief,
since I do purpose to marry, I will think nothing
to any purpose that the world can say against it;
and therefore never flout at me for what I have
said against it; for man is a giddy thing, and this
is my conclusion. For thy part, Claudio, I did 110
think to have beaten thee; but in that thou art
like to be my kinsman, live unbruised, and love
my cousin.

Claud. I had well hoped thou wouldst have denied
Beatrice, that I might have cudgelled thee out
of thy single life, to make thee a double-dealer;
which, out of question, thou wilt be, if my cousin
do not look exceeding narrowly to thee.

Bene. Come, come, we are friends: let's have a dance
ere we are married, that we may lighten our 120
own hearts, and our wives' heels.

Leon. We'll have dancing afterward.

Bene. First, of my word; therefore play, music.
Prince, thou art sad; get thee a wife, get thee a
wife: there is no staff more reverend than one
tipped with horn.

Enter a Messenger.

Mess. My lord, your brother John is ta'en in flight,
    And brought with armed men back to Messina.
Bene. Think not on him till to-morrow: I'll devise
    thee brave punishments for him. Strike up, 130
    pipers.   [*Dance. Exeunt.*

Glossary.

ABUSED, deceived ; V. ii. 100.

ACCORDANT, favourable ; I. ii. 14.

ADAM ; alluding to the outlaw Adam Bell, famous as an archer (cp. Percy's Reliques). I. i. 261.

ADVERTISEMENT, moral instruction ; V. i. 32.

AFEARD, afraid ; II. iii. 158.

AFFECT, love ; I. i. 298.

AFFECTION, desire ; II, ii. 6.

AFTER, afterwards ; I. i. 328.

AGATE ; an allusion to the little figures cut in agates, often worn in rings ; a symbol of smallness ; III. i. 65.

AIM ; "a. better at me," form a better opinion of me ; II. ii. 99.

ALLIANCE ; "Good Lord for al." i.e. "Heaven send me a husband," or "Good Lord, how many alliances are forming !" ; II. i. 330.

ALMS ; "an alms" = a charity ; II. iii. 164.

ANCIENTRY, old fashioned manners ; II. i. 80.

ANGEL, a gold coin (with pun upon noble and angel, both coins) ; II. iii. 35.

ANSWER ; "to your a." i.e. "to answer for your conduct" ; V. i. 233.

ANTIQUE, antic, buffoon ; III. i. 63.

ANTIQUELY, fantastically ; V. i. 96.

APES ; a reference to the old superstition that old maids had to lead apes in hell ; II. i. 43.

APPEAR ITSELF, appear as a reality ; I. ii. 22.

APPREHENSION ; "professed ap." i.e. "set up for a wit" ; III. iv. 68.

APPROVED, tried, proved ; II. i. 394 ; IV. i. 45.

ARGUMENT, subject (for satire) ; I. i. 258 ; proof ; II. iii. 243.

AT A WORD = in a word ; II. i. 118.

ATE, goddess of Fury and Mischief ; II. i. 263.

BALDRICK, belt ; I. i. 244.

BEAR IN HAND, keep in (false) hope ; IV. i. 305.

BEAR-WARD (Quartos, Folios, read berrord ; other eds., bear-herd), bear-leader ; II. i. 43.

BEATEN ; "b. with brains," i.e mocked ; V. iv. 104.

BEL ; "God Bel's priests" alludes to some representation in stained glass of the story of Bel and the Dragon ; III. iii. 143.

BELOW STAIRS ; "shall I always keep below stairs," an expression of doubtful meaning ; probably = "in the servant's room" ; hence "remain unmarried" ; V. ii. 10.

BENT, tension, straining (properly an expression of archery) ; II. iii. 232 ; disposition ; IV. i. 188.

BILLS ; "set up his bills," i.e. "posted his challenge, like a fencing-master" ; I. i. 39.

BILLS, pikes carried by watchmen ; III. iii. 43.

BILLS, used quibblingly for (1) bonds, and (2) watchmen's halberds ; III. iii. 191.

BIRD-BOLT, a short arrow with a broad flat end, used to kill birds without piercing ; I. i, 42.

125

BLACK, dark-complexioned; III. i. 63.

BLAZON, explanation; II. i. 307.

BLOCK, wooden model for shaping hats; I. i. 77.

BLOOD, temperament; I. iii. 29; passion; II. i. 187.

BLOODS, young fellows; III. iii. 141.

BOARDED, accosted; II. i. 149.

BOOKS; "not in your books," i.e. "not in your good books"; I. i. 79.

BORROWS; "b. money in God's name," i.e. "begs it"; V. i. 319.

BOTTLE, a small wooden barrel; I. i. 259.

BRAVE, becoming, fitting; IV. v. 130.

BREAK, broach the subject; I. i. 311, 328.

BREATHING = breathing-space; II. i. 378.

BRING, accompany; III. ii. 3.

BUCKLERS; "I give thee the b." i.e. "I yield thee the victory"; V. ii. 17.

BY, concerning; V. i. 312.

CANDLE-WASTERS, those who burn the midnight oil, bookworms; V. i. 18.

CANKER, canker-rose; I. iii. 28.

CAPON, used as a term of contempt; (? a pun, according to some = "a fool's cap on"); V. i. 156.

CARDUUS; "C. Benedictus," the holy-thistle; a plant supposed to cure all diseases, including the plague; III. iv. 73.

CARE KILLED A CAT, an old proverbial expression; V. i. 132.

CAREER; "in the c." i.e. "in tilting, as at a tournament"; V. i. 135.

CARPET-MONGERS, carpet-knights; V. ii. 32.

CARRIAGE, bearing, deportment; I. iii. 30.

CARRY, carry out; II. iii. 223.

CARVING, modelling, fashioning; II. iii. 18.

CENSURED, judged; II. iii. 233.

CHARGE, burden; I. i. 103; commission, office; III. iii. 7.

CHEAPEN, bid for; II. iii. 33.

CINQUE-PACE, a lively kind of dance; II. i. 77, 82.

CIRCUMSTANCES; "c. shortened," i.e. "to omit details"; III. ii. 105.

CIVET, a perfume made from the civet-cat; III. ii. 50.

CIVIL, used quibblingly with a play upon "civil" and "Seville"; II. i. 304.

CLAW, flatter; I. iii. 19.

COG, to deceive, especially by smooth lies; V. i. 95.

COIL; confusion, III. iii. 100; old coil = much ado, great stir, "the devil to pay"; V. ii. 98.

COLDLY, quietly; III. ii. 132.

COMMODITY, any kind of merchandise; III. iii. 190.

COMPANY, companionship; V. i. 192.

COMPREHENDED, blunder for "apprehended"; III. v. 50.

CONCEIT, conception; II. i. 309.

CONDITIONS, qualities; III. ii. 68.

CONFIRMED, unmoved; V. iv. 17.

CONSUMMATE, consummated; III. ii. 1.

CONTEMPTIBLE, contemptuous; II. iii. 188.

CONTROLMENT, constraint; I. iii. 21.

CONVEYANCE; "impossible c." incredible dexterity; II. i. 252.

COUNT COMFECT, i.e. "Count Sugarplum," with probably a play upon conte or compte, a fictitious story; IV. i. 318.

COUNTIES, counts; IV. i. 317.

COUNTY, count; II. i. 195; II. 1 370.

COURTESIES, mere forms of courtesy; IV. i. 322.

COURTESY = curtsey; II. i. 56.

COUSINS, kinsmen, enrolled among the dependants of great families, little more than attendants; I. ii. 25.

CROSS; "broke c." i.e. "broke a-

THWART the opponent's body"; (an expression taken from tilting) V. i. 139.

CUNNING, clever; V. i. 234.

CURST, shrewish; II. i. 22, 23, &c.

DAFF, put off; V. i. 78.

DAFFED, put aside; II. iii. 176.

DANGEROUS, threatening; V. i. 97.

DEADLY, mortally; V. i. 178.

DEAR HAPPINESS, a precious piece of good fortune; I. i. 129.

DECERNS=a blunder for "concerns"; III. v. 4.

DEFEND, forbid; II. i. 97.

DEFILED (the reading of the Quartos, omitted in the Folio), defiled by slander; V. iv. 63.

DEPRAVE, practise detraction; V. i. 95.

DIFFERENCE, used technically; "heraldic differences" distinguish the bearers of the same coat armour, and demonstrate their nearness to the representative of the family; I. i. 69.

DISCOVER, reveal; III. ii. 96.

DISCOVERED, revealed; I. ii. 11.

DIVISION, order, arrangement; V. i. 229.

DOCTOR, a learned person; V. i. 206.

DON WORM (Conscience was formerly represented under the symbol of a worm); V. ii. 86.

DOTAGE, doting love; II. iii. 175, 224.

DOUBLE-DEALER, one who is unfaithful in love or wedlock; V. iv. 116.

DOUBLET AND HOSE; "in his d. and h." *i.e.* "without his cloak"; alluding to the custom of taking off the cloak before fighting a duel; V. i. 203.

DOUBT, suspect; V. i. 118.

DRAW, draw the bow of a fiddle (according to others draw the instruments from their cases); V. i. 128.

DROVIER=drover; II. i. 201.

DRY HAND (a sign of a cold and chaste nature); II. i. 123.

DUMB-SHOW, a pantomime; II. iii. 226.

DUMPS, low spirits; II. iii. 73.

EARNEST, handsel, part payment; II. i. 42.

ECSTASY, madness; II. iii. 157.

EFTEST, quickest (perhaps a blunder for "deftest"); IV. ii. 38.

EMBASSAGE, embassy; I. i. 282.

ENGAGED, pledged; IV. i. 335.

ENTERTAINED, employed; I. iii. 60.

EUROPA, Europe (used quibblingly); V. iv. 45-6.

EVEN, plain; IV. i. 266.

EVERY DAY, immediately, without delay, as the French *incessamment*; perhaps "E. to-morrow"="every day (after) to-morrow"; III. i. 101.

EXCOMMUNICATION, blunder for "communication"; III. v. 69.

EXHIBITION; "e. to examine," possibly a blunder for "examination to exhibit"; IV. ii. 5.

EXPERIMENTAL; "e. seal" *i.e.* "the seal of experience"; IV. i. 168.

FAITH, fidelity in friendship; I. i. 75; honour, pledge; IV. i. 8.

FANCY, love; III. ii. 31.

FASHION-MONGING, foppish; V. i. 94.

FATHERS HERSELF, is like her father; I. i. 112.

FAVOUR, countenance; II. i. 97.

FENCE, skill in fencing; V. i. 75.

FESTIVAL TERMS, not in everyday language; II. i. 41.

FETCH ME IN, draw me into a confession; I. i. 225.

FINE, conclusion; I. i. 247.

FLEER, sneer; V. i. 58.

FLEET, company; II. i. 148.

FLIGHT, shooting with the flight, a kind of light and well-feathered arrow; I. i. 40.

FLOUT; "f. old ends," *i.e.* make fun of old endings of letters; I. i. 290.

FLOUTING JACK, mocking rascal; I. i. 186.

FOINING, thrusting; V. i. 84.

FRAME, order, disposition of things; IV. i. 130.

FRAMED, devised; V. i. 71.

FROM, away from; "f. all fashions," averse to all fashions, eccentric; III. i. 72.

FULL; "you have it full," *i.e.* "you are fully answered"; I. i. 110.

FULL, fully; III. i. 45.

FURNISH, to dress; III. i. 103.

GIRDLE; "to turn his girdle," to give a challenge (alluding to the practice of turning the large buckle of the girdle behind one, previously to challenging anyone); V. i. 142.

GOD SAVE THE FOUNDATION! (the customary phrase employed by those who received alms at the gates of religious houses); V. i. 327.

GO IN = join with you in; I. i. 188.

GOOD DEN, good evening; III. ii. 83.

GOOD-YEAR, supposed to be a corruption of *goujère*, a disease; used as a mild imprecation; I. iii. 1.

GO TO THE WORLD, to marry; II. i. 330.

GRACE, favour; I. iii. 23.

GRACIOUS, attractive; IV. i. 109.

GRANT; the fairest grant = "the best boon is that which answers the necessities of the case"; I. i. 319.

GREAT CHAM, the Khan of Tartary; II. i. 277.

GUARDED, ornamented; I. i. 288.

GUARDS, ornaments; I. i. 289.

GUERDON, recompense; V. iii. 5.

H, *i.e. ache*; the latter word and the name of the letter were pronounced alike; III. iv. 56.

HAGGARDS, wild, untrained hawks; III. i. 36.

HALF-PENCE, very small pieces; II. iii. 146.

HAPPINESS; "outward happiness," *i.e.* "prepossessing appearance"; II. iii. 190.

HARE-FINDER, one skilled to find the hare; with perhaps a play upon "hair-finder"; I. i. 186.

HEAD, "to thy head" = "to thy face"; V. i. 62.

HEARKEN AFTER, inquire into; V. i. 216.

"HEIGH-HO FOR A HUSBAND," the title of an old ballad still extant (*cp.* III. iv. 54, 55); II. i. 332.

HEIGHT, highest degree; IV. i. 303.

HIGH-PROOF, in a high degree; V. i. 123.

HOBBY-HORSES (used as a term of contempt); III. ii. 75.

HOLD IT UP, continue it; II. iii. 126.

HOLDS; "h. you well," thinks well of you; III. ii. 101.

HOW, however; III. i. 60.

"HUNDRED MERRY TALES," a popular jest-book of the time (included in Hazlitt's Collection of Shakespeare Jest Books, 1864); II. i. 135.

IMPORTANT, importunate; II. i. 74.

IMPOSE ME TO, impose upon me; V. i. 282.

IN, with; II. i. 68.

INCENSED, instigated; V. i. 242.

INFINITE, infinite stretch, utmost power; II. iii. 106.

IN RESPECT OF = in comparison with; III. iv. 18.

INTEND, pretend; II. ii. 35.

IN THAT, inasmuch as; V. iv. 111.

INVENTION, mental activity; IV. i. 196.

INWARDNESS, intimacy; IV. i. 247.

JACKS (used as a term of contempt); V. i. 91.

JUST, that is so; II. i. 29.

KID-FOX, young fox; II. iii. 44.

KIND, natural; I. i. 26.

KINDLY, natural; IV. i. 75.

LAPWING, a reference to the habit of the female green plover; when disturbed on its nest it runs close to the ground a short distance without uttering any cry, while the male bird keeps flying round the intruder, uttering its peculiar cry very rapidly and loudly, and trying, by every means, to draw him in a contrary direction from the nest; III. i. 24.

LARGE, "large jests," broad jests; II. iii. 206.

LARGE, free, licentious; IV. i. 53.

LEAF'D, covered; V. iv. 49.

LEARN, teach; IV. i. 31.

LEWD, depraved; V. i. 341.

LIBERAL, licentious; IV. i. 93.

LIGHT o' LOVE, a popular old dance tune, often referred to; III. iv. 44.

LIMED, snared as with bird-lime; III. i. 104.

LIVER (used as "heart" for the seat of love); IV. i. 233.

LOCK, a love-lock; III. iii. 183.

LOCK; "he wears a key in his ear, and a l. hanging by it," a quibbling allusion to the "love-locks" worn at the time, and perhaps to the fashion of wearing roses in the ears; V. i. 318.

LODGE, the hut occupied by the watchman in a rabbit-warren; II. i. 222.

LOW, short; III. i. 65.

LUSTIHOOD, vigour; V. i. 76.

LUXURIOUS, lustful; IV. i. 42.

MARCH-CHICK, chicken hatched in March, denoting precocity; I. iii. 58.

MARL, a kind of clay; II. i. 66.

MATCH, mate, marry; II. i. 68.

MATTER, sense, seriousness; II. i. 344.

MATTER, "no such matter," nothing of the kind; II. iii. 225.

MAY, can; IV. i. 267.

MEASURE, used quibblingly in double sense in connection with dance; II. i. 74.

MEDICINABLE, medicinal; II. ii. 5.

MEET WITH, even with; I. i. 47.

MERELY, entirely; II. iii. 226.

METAL, material; II. i. 62.

MISGOVERNMENT, misconduct; IV. i. 100.

MISPRISING, despising; III. i. 52.

MISPRISION, mistake; IV. i. 187.

MISUSE, deceive; II. ii. 28.

MISUSED, abused; II. i. 246.

MOE, more; II. iii. 72.

MONUMENT; "in m." = "in men's memory"; V. ii. 81.

MORAL, hidden meaning, like the moral of a fable; III. iv. 78.

MORAL, ready to moralize; V. i. 30.

MORTIFYING, killing; III. i. 13.

MOUNTAIN, a great heap, a huge amount; III. i. 382.

MOUNTANTO, i.e. montanto, a term in fencing, "an upright blow or thrust," applied by Beatrice to Benedict; I. i. 30.

NEAR, dear to; II. i. 169.

NEIGHBOURS; the time of "good n." i.e. "when men were not envious of one another"; V. ii. 79.

NEW-TROTHED, newly betrothed; III. i. 38.

NIGHT-GOWN, dressing gown; III. iv. 18.

NIGHT-RAVEN, the owl or the nightheron; II. iii. 84.

NONCOME; "to a n." probably = to be *non compos mentis*; III. v. 67.

NOTHING, pronounced much in the same way as "noting"; hence the pun here on "no-thing" and "noting"; II. iii. 59.

NUPTIAL, marriage ceremony; IV. i. 69.

OF, by; I. i. 126.

OFF, away from; III. v. 10.

ON, of; IV. i. 139.

ONLY, alone, of all others; I. iii. 41.

OPINIONED, a blunder for "pinioned"; IV. ii. 69.

ORCHARD, garden; I. ii. 10.

ORTHOGRAPHY = orthographer, one who uses fine words; II. iii. 21.

OUT-FACING, facing the matter out with looks; V. i. 94.

OVER-BORNE, overcome; II. iii. 157.

PACK'D, implicated; V. i. 308.

PALABRAS, *i.e. pocas palabras,* (Spanish) = "few words"; III. v. 18.

PARTRIDGE WING (formerly considered the most delicate part of the bird); II. i. 155.

PASSING, exceedingly; II. i. 84.

PASSION, emotion; V. i. 23.

PENT-HOUSE, a porch or shed with sloping roof; III. iii. 110.

PHILEMON'S ROOF; an allusion to the story of the peasant Philemon and his Baucis, who received Jupiter into their thatched cottage; II. i. 99.

PIETY, Dogberry's blunder for "impiety"; IV. ii. 81.

PIGMIES, a race of dwarfs fabled to dwell beyond Mount Imaus in India; II. i. 278.

PIKES, central spikes screwed into the bucklers or shields, of the 16th century; V. ii. 21.

PITCH; "they that touch pitch, &c.," a popular proverb derived from

Ecclesiasticus xiii. 1; III. iii. 60.

PLEACHED, interwoven; III. i. 7.

PLEASANT, merry; I. i. 37.

PLUCK UP, rouse thyself; V. i. 207.

POSSESS, inform; V. i. 290.

POSSESSED, influenced; III. iii. 166.

PRACTICE, contrivance, plotting; IV. i. 190.

PRECEPTIAL; "p. medicine," *i.e.* "the medicine of precepts"; V. i. 24.

PRESENT, represent; III. iii. 79.

PRESENTLY, immediately; II. ii. 57.

PRESS; an allusion to the punishment known as the *peine forte et dure,* which consisted of piling heavy weights on the body; II. i. 76.

PRESTER JOHN, Presbyter John, a mythical Christian King of India, of whose wonders Mandeville tells us much; II. i. 276.

PRIZED, estimated; III. i. 90.

PROHIBIT (used amiss by Dogberry); V. i. 336.

PROLONG'D, deferred; IV. i. 256.

PROOF; "your own p." *i.e.* "in your own trial of her"; IV. i. 46.

PROPER, handsome; III. iii. 189.

PROPEREST, handsomest; V. i. 174.

PROPOSE, conversation; III. i. 12.

PROPOSING, conversing; III. i. 3.

PUSH; "made a push at," *i.e.* "defied"; V. i. 38.

QUALIFY, moderate; V. iv. 67.

QUEASY, squeamish; II. i. 399.

QUESTION; "in q." *i.e.* "under trial, subject to judicial examination"; III. iii. 192.

QUESTION = that's the question; V. ii. 84.

QUESTION, investigation; V. iv. 6.

QUIPS, sarcasms; II. iii. 249.

QUIRKS, shallow conceits; II. iii. 245.

QUIT, requite; IV. i. 202.

RABATO, collar, ruff ; III. iv. 6.

RACK, stretch, exaggerate ; IV. i. 222.

REASONS (punning, according to some commentators, upon "reasons" and "raisins") ; V. i. 211.

RECHEAT, a term of the chase ; the call sounded to bring the dogs back ; I. i. 242.

RECLUSIVE, secluded : IV. i. 244.

REDEMPTION, a blunder for "perdition" ; IV. ii. 59.

REECHY, reeky, dirty ; III. iii. 143.

REFORMED, Dogberry's blunder for *informed* ; V. i. 262.

REMORSE, compassion ; IV. i. 213.

RENDER, give back ; IV. i. 30.

REPORTINGLY, on mere report ; III. i. 116.

REPROVE, disprove ; II. iii. 241.

REVERENCE, privilege of age ; V. i. 64.

RHEUM, tears ; V. ii. 85.

RIGHT ; " do me right," give me satisfaction ; V. i. 149.

SAD, serious ; I. i. 185 ; I. iii. 62 ; II. i. 358-9.

SADLY, seriously ; II. iii. 229.

SALVED, palliated ; I. i. 317.

SATURN ; "born under S." *i.e.* "of a saturnine or phlegmatic disposition" ; I. iii. 12.

SCAB, used quibblingly for (1) sore, and (2) a low fellow ; III. iii. 107.

SCAMBLING, scrambling ; V. i. 94.

SEEMING, hypocrisy ; IV. i. 57.

SELF-ENDEARED, self-loving ; III. i. 56.

SENTENCES, sententious sayings ; II. iii. 249.

SEVEN-NIGHT, "a just s." *i.e.* "exactly a week" ; II. i. 375.

SHAVEN HERCULES, probably alludes to Hercules, shaved to look like a woman, while in the service of Omphale ; III. iii. 145.

SHREWD, shrewish ; II. i. 20.

SIDE, long ; III. iv. 20.

SIGH ; "sigh away Sundays," possibly an allusion to the Puritans' Sabbath ; according to others the phrase signifies that a man has no rest at all ; I. i. 204.

SLANDERS, misapplied by Dogberry for "slanderers" ; V. i. 221

SLOPS, large loose breeches ; III. ii. 36.

SMIRCHED, soiled ; III. iii. 145.

SMOKING, fumigating ; I. iii. 61

SO, if ; II. i. 91.

SOFT YOU, hold, stop ; V. i. 207.

SORT, rank ; I. i. 7 ; I. i. 33.

SORT, turn out ; V. iv. 7.

SPEED'S, *i.e.* speed us ; V. iii. 32.

SPELL ; "s. him backward," misconstrue him ; III. i. 61.

SQUARER, quarreller ; I. i. 82.

STAFF, lance ; V. i. 138.

STALE, harlot ; IV. i. 66.

STALK, walk, like a fowler behind a stalking-horse ; II. iii. 95.

START-UP, up-start ; I. iii. 68.

STOMACH, appetite ; I. iii. 16.

STOPS, the divisions on the finger-board of a lute ; III. ii. 62.

STRAIN, family, lineage ; II. i. 394.

STRAIN ; "strain for strain," *i.e.* feeling for feeling ; V. i. 12.

STYLE (used with a quibble on "stile") ; V. ii. 6.

SUCCESS, the issue ; IV. i. 236.

SUFFERANCE, suffering ; V. i. 38.

SUFFIGANCE, blunder for "sufficient" ; III. v. 56.

SUN-BURNT, homely, ill-favoured ; II. i. 331.

SURE, faithful ; I. iii. 71.

SUSPECT, misapplied for "respect" ; IV. ii. 76, 77.

SUSPICION (*i.e.* suspicion of having horns under it) ; I. i. 201.

SWIFT, ready ; III. i. 89,

TAKEN UP, used quibblingly for (1) arrested, and (2) obtained on credit; III. iii. 191.

TALE; "both in a tale," *i.e.* "they both say the same"; IV. ii. 33.

TAX, to censure; I. i. 46.

TEACH, to be taught; I. i. 293.

TEMPER, compound, mix; II. ii. 21.

TEMPORIZE, make terms; I. i. 276.

TERMINATIONS, terms; II. i. 256.

THICK-PLEACHED, thickly intervowen; I. ii. 9.

TICKLING (trisyllabic); III. i. 80.

TIRE, head-dress; III. iv. 13.

TO, with; II. i. 243.

TONGUES; "he hath the t." *i.e.* "he knows foreign languages"; V. i. 167.

TO-NIGHT, last night; III. v. 33.

TOOTH-PICKER = tooth-pick; II. i. 274.

TOP; "by the top" = by the forelock; I. ii. 15.

TRACE, walk; III. i. 16.

TRANS-SHAPE, caricature; V. i. 172.

TRIAL; "to trial of a man," *i.e.* "to a combat, man to man"; V. i. 66.

TROW = trow ye, *i.e.* think ye? III. iv. 59.

TRUTH, genuine proof; II. ii. 49.

TUITION, guardianship; I. i. 283.

TURNED TURK = completely changed for the worse; III. iv. 57.

TYRANT, pitiless censor; I. i. 170.

UNCONFIRMED, inexperienced; III. iii. 124.

UNDERBORNE, trimmed, faced; III. iv. 21.

UNDERGOES, is subject to; V. ii. 57.

UNHAPPINESS, wanton or mischievous tricks; II. i. 361.

UNTOWARDLY, unluckily; III. ii. 134.

UP AND DOWN, exactly; II. i. 123.

UPON, in consequence of; IV. i. 225.

USE, usury, interest; I. i. 288.

USED; "hath u." *i.e.* has made a practice of; used equivocally; V. i. 320.

USURER'S CHAIN, an allusion to the gold chains worn by the more wealthy merchants, many of whom were bankers; II. i. 196.

VAGROM, Dogberry's blunder for vagrant; III. i. 25.

VENICE, the city of pleasure-seekers, frequently alluded to as such by Elizabethan writers; I. i. 274.

WEAK, foolish; III. i. 54.

WEEDS, garments, dress; V. iii. 30.

WINDY; "on the w. side of care," *i.e.* "to windward of care" (the metaphor being from two sailing boats racing); II. i. 327.

WISH, desire; III. i. 42.

WIT, wisdom; II. iii. 194.

WITH = by; II. i. 64; V. iv. 128.

WITS; "five wits," *i.e.* "the five intellectual powers, — common wit, imagination, fantasy, estimation, memory"; I. i. 66.

WOE, woful tribute; V. iii. 33.

WOO, press; II. iii. 50.

WOODCOCK, fool; V. i. 158.

WOOLLEN, blankets; II. i. 33.

WRING, writhe; V. i. 28.

Notes.

I. i. 218. The English story of "Mr Fox" alluded to here was first written down by Blakeway, who contributed to Malone's Variorum Edition a version of the tale he had heard from an old aunt (*cp.* Jacobs' *English Fairy Tales*).

II. i. 221. "*As melancholy as a lodge in a warren*": the phrase suggests "The daughter of Zion is left as a cottage in a vineyard, as a lodge in a garden of cucumbers," Isaiah i. 8.

II. ii. 45. Some editors substitute "Borachio" for "Claudio" in order to relieve the difficulty here, but, as the Cambridge editors point out, "Hero's supposed offence would not be enhanced by calling one lover by the name of the other. . . . Perhaps the author meant that Borachio should persuade her to play, as children say, at being Hero and Claudio."

II. iii. 38. The Folio reads :—" *Enter Prince, Leonato, Claudio, and Jack Wilson*": the latter was probably the singer who took the part of Balthasar.

III. ii. 27. "*Where is but a humour or a worm*": toothache was popularly supposed to be caused by a worm at the root of the tooth.

III. iii. It is an interesting fact that "Dogberry," the vulgar name of the *dogwood*, was used as a surname as far back as the time of Richard II., and that "Verges," a provincial corruption or *verjuice*, occurs in an ancient MS. (MS. Ashmol. 38) as the name of a usurer whose epitaph is given:—

> "Here lies father Varges
>   Who died to save charges."

III. iii. 92. "*Keep your fellows' counsels and your own.*" It has been pointed out by students of Shakespeare's legal acquirements that these words still form part of the oath administered by judges' marshal to the grand jurymen at the present day.

III. v. 18. "*Comparisons are odorous.*" An elaborate extension of this joke occurs in the old play of *Sir Gyles Goosecappe* (c. 1603).

III. v. 37. "*When the age is in, the wit is out*"; a blunder for the old proverbial expression, "when the ale is in, wit is out"—

> "When ale is in, wit is out,
>   When ale is out, wit is in,
> The first thou showest out of doubt,
>   The last in thee hath not been."
>   HEYWOOD's *Epigrams and Proverbs.*

IV. ii. Nearly all the speeches of Dogberry throughout the scene are given to the famous comedian "Kemp," those of Verges to "Cowley." William Kemp and Richard Cowley are among the "principall actors" enumerated in the First Folio. The retention of the names of the actors "supplies a measure of the editorial care to which the several Folios were submitted." Dogberry's speech is assigned to "*Andrew*," probably a familiar appellation of Kemp, who, according to the Cambridge Edition, often played the part of "Merry Andrew."

IV. ii. 5. "*We have the exhibition to examine.*" Verges' blunder is not quite clear: possibly "exhibition" is used in the sense of "allowance" or permission; otherwise he perhaps means "examination to exhibit."

V. i. 16. "*Bid sorrow wag, cry 'hem'!*" The Quarto and the first and second Folios read, "*And sorrow wagge, crie hem*": Folio 3, "*And hallow, wag, cry hem*": Folio 4, "*And hollow, wag, cry hem.*" Many emendations have been suggested. Capell's "*bid sorrow wag,*" is now generally adopted. Johnson proposed "*Cry, sorrow wag! and hem.*" ("Sorrow wag," like "care away," was probably a proverbial phrase.) One other suggestion is perhaps noteworthy :—"*And, sorry wag, cry 'hem.'*"

V. iii. 20, 21. "*Heavily, heavily*"; so reads the Quarto; the Folios "*Heavenly, heavenly,*" adopted by many editors. The same error, however, of "*heavenly*" for "*heavily*" occurs in the Folio reading of *Hamlet* II. ii. 309.

"The slayers of the virgin knight are performing a solemn requiem on the body of Hero, and they invoke Midnight and the shades of the dead to assist, until *her* death be *uttered*, that is, proclaimed, published, sorrowfully, sorrowfully " (Halliwell).

V. iv. 125. "*There is no staff more reverend than one tipped with horn*"; *i.e.* having a ferrule of horn; there is, of course, a quibbling allusion in the words to the favourite Elizabethan joke.